N
W   E
S

Old
Pierr

Ahwun

L. HURON

Georgian Bay

L. ONTARIO

Ft.
Niagara

Ft.
Detroit

L. ERIE

Sir
Jeffrey

D0619509

The Young Voyageur

The Young Voyageur

By DIRK GRINGHUIS *

MACKINAC STATE HISTORIC PARKS

THE YOUNG VOYAGEUR

Library of Congress Catalog Card Number: 55-7279
PUBLISHED BY MACKINAC STATE HISTORIC PARKS
Printed in the United States of America

Revised edition	1969	5000 copies
Second printing	1973	5000 copies
Third printing	1979	7500 copies
Fourth printing	1988	3000 copies
Fifth printing	1991	3000 copies
Sixth printing	1994	3000 copies
Seventh printing	1996	6000 copies

Printed by The John Henry Co.
Lansing, Michigan 48906

To Helen

Contents

Indian Words
Used in This Story

Ahwun Ogemahqua, Ah-wun O-geh-mah-qua: Woman
  of the Mist
Bahwetig, Bah-weh-tig: Woman of the Rapids
Boozhoo, Boo-zoo: Greetings
Gebwahnuhsins, Geb-wah-nuh-sins: Little Hawk
Howh, How: Yes
Mahgwah or Mukwah, Mah-gwa or Muk-wa: Bear
Mahnahdud, Mah-nah-dud: Bad
Meno, Men-o: Good
Michilimackinac, Mich-ill-ih-mack-in-aw: Land of the
  Great Turtle
Misquah, Mis-qua: Red-headed One
Nanabojo, Na-na-bo-zho: Indian God of Fair Weather
Pakkosigon, Pak-ko-sih-gon: Indian Tobacco
Peepaukawis, Pee-pawk-a-wis: Evil Brother of Nanabojo
Sawaquot, Sa-wa-qwat: Fork-in-the-Tree
Wahbeatik, Wah-beh-a-tik: White Elk
Wahbunoong, Wah-bu-noong: Woman from the East

The Young Voyageur

Bear Tracks

DANNY O'HARA sat astraddle the top rail of his father's fence. At his feet a wooden bucket of feed lay forgotten while from the pigpen, Chief Pontiac stood grunting his displeasure.

Young Danny didn't budge. Blue eyes intent under his shock of red hair, he stared across the fields at the walls of Fort Detroit. Suddenly he leaned forward. There was a bright flash, a puff of smoke. The dull boom of a six-pounder echoed across the cleared land.

Danny grinned. He swung one long leg over the rail and dropped easily to the ground. He had won!

It was his favorite game and he played it nightly. If he failed to hear and see the evening gun signaling the closing of the gates, the next day he had to be a farmer. But if he saw the flash he could pretend he was a real *voyageur* like his friend Jacques Le Blanc.

The year was 1762. What had been French Canada, all of the country between the Ohio and the Great Lakes, all of the land in the St. Lawrence Valley, belonged to the British Crown. Small detachments of Royal Americans garrisoned the forts built by the French. Major Robert Rogers, leader of the famous Rangers, had hauled down the Lilies of France and had hoisted the Cross of Saint George at Forts Niagara, Venango, Presque-Isle, and Le Boeuf to the east; La Hayes, St. Joseph, and Michilimackinac on Lake Michigan; Sandusky, Miami, and Detroit on the shores of Lake Erie. So in spite of Rogers' warnings of a new threat in Pontiac, great war chief of the Ottawas, it seemed as though peace had come to the Colonies at last.

Danny O'Hara caught up the bucket of feed and strode to the pigpen. Chief Pontiac was waiting, small angry eyes peering up at Danny through the rain.

"Here you are, Chief." Danny flung the contents of the pail into the trough. "Good American food to keep you fat and peaceful."

Watching, Danny remembered the time a year ago when he and his father, late of Rogers' Rangers, and his mother had settled at Fort Detroit. The pig had been left there by a French-Canadian farmer who had fled at the approach of Rogers' whaleboats. His father had taken one look at the pig and dubbed him "Chief Pontiac." "Faith, and he looks savage enough," the O'Hara had said. Danny's mother had objected. "Is that the way for you to be talkin' in front of the boy?" she had asked. "He'll be learnin' about the Indians soon enough," the O'Hara had answered.

Danny shook his head. How was he going to learn about anything, spending all his time working the farm? He wished they lived in the fort like Meeker the trader and the other colonists. There was excitement inside the walls. Troops drilling, Indians bringing furs, voyageurs loading north canoes for the trip up the lakes to Fort Michilimackinac, the land of the Great Turtle. If only the O'Hara had gone into trading as Silas Meeker had done. Then Danny might have a "light canoe" of his own. He would paint a picture of a deer or maybe a bear on the bow as the voyageurs did.

Danny straightened and pointed an imaginary musket at the black sides of Chief Pontiac. "Pow!" Danny stepped back, feeling the imaginary kick of the stock against his shoulder. He lowered the smoking musket, picked up the empty bucket, and started for the house. Danny O'Hara, voyageur, had killed another bear.

He stopped. Something was moving along the far side of the house. Was it a shadow, an animal, or a prowling Indian? Heart pounding, the bucket still in his hand, Danny hesitated. All of the stories his father had been telling came back to him. Stories of painted savages with gleaming hatchets creeping up on unwary settlers; of massacres, burned cabins, scalpings . . . Danny shivered.

The shadow moved again. Danny raised the bucket and flung it straight at the dark object. The bucket hit the wall with a rattling thud and Danny sprinted for the house. There was a loud snort. Jerking open the door, Danny glanced back just in time to see something loping off into the darkness. For a moment he thought that Chief Pontiac was loose from his pen. Then he knew. The shadow was a bear!

"Pa!" Danny slammed the door behind him and dropped the bar. "Pa, I saw something. . . ."

The O'Hara, half asleep, nearly fell from his chair. "What's that? Faith now, and what did ye see?"

"A bear, Pa. A real live bear! I threw my bucket at him."

"Where's me musket?" The O'Hara, his face a bright pink, white hair standing straight up like splints on a new birch broom, limped rapidly to the fireplace. He jerked down his musket, powder horn, and shot pouch. "Now open the door, Danny, and we'll be havin' a look."

"Yes, sir." Danny lifted the bar, his hands trembling with excitement. Danny felt his mother's hand on his shoulder.

"Mind now that you're careful," she said.

"Don't be worryin', Mary." The O'Hara pulled open the door. "Sure and I'm not afraid of man nor beast."

With a bound he was outside, the flintlock cocked and ready. Danny was close behind him. All at once he grabbed his father's arm.

"There, over there. . . ."

The musket roared.

"Fetch me a lantern, boy, and be quick." Already the O'Hara was pouring powder into the muzzle and pan of the smoking musket.

Danny saw his mother's pale face.

"Here, take the Betty lamp," she said.

Danny held the lamp high, shielding the flickering flame. He heard his father snort. Danny peered closer. On the ground lay the feed bucket, a gaping hole drilled straight through the bottom.

"A bucket!" The O'Hara turned in disgust.

From the door came a smothered giggle.

"That will do, woman." The O'Hara marched stiffly to the fireplace and returned the musket to the pegs. "As for you, Daniel O'Hara, the next time you see a bear, will you do me the favor of forgettin' it?"

"But I saw one, Pa, honest. . . ."

His mother, eyes twinkling, was ladling mush into wooden bowls. "Now let's be sittin' down to supper. Glad I am that your father is not afraid of man nor beast nor buckets."

"You can joke all you like, Mary," the O'Hara said. "But supposin' that bucket had been one of Pontiac's painted divils. Would ye have laughed then?" Triumphantly, the O'Hara sat down and attacked his mush.

"I did think it was an Indian at first, Pa," Danny said.

"And well you might, Danny. Pontiac is stirrin' up the tribes. And mind what I say. The British are not helpin' a bit. Treatin' the Indians like dogs, they are worse than us Americans. And who was it that saved their precious hides in the French War? The Americans. Virginians under Washington, Rogers' Rangers, while General Braddock kept on marchin' his fine redcoats on parade so's the Indians could pick 'em off like partridge on a fence rail."

"Now, Michael, I'm that tired of war. Peace has come to the Colonies and I want to be forgettin' the old fears."

"Forget 'em you can't, Mary. Peace isn't so easy and I wish you would be reconsiderin' my plea to move into the fort."

"Oh, 'tis movin' into the fort you want? Wouldn't be because you're tired of farmin' and would like to be a storekeeper, O'Hara?"

"And why not?" Danny's father said. "Sure and you'd be havin' some pretties if we had a store. Think of that!" He winked at Danny.

"Go way with you and your blarney, O'Hara. We're stayin' here. At least we have enough to eat. You know what would happen if we were livin' at the fort. Talkin' and tellin' tales you'd be, instead of tendin' to business. And what's more, I'll not be havin' Danny hangin' about with the riffraff as calls themselves voy'jers or some such heathen name."

"It's voyageurs, Ma," Danny said. "And they aren't riffraff. Look at Jacques Le Blanc."

"I'll not be discussin' it. Besides, where would we be gettin' money to stock a store, O'Hara?"

"Now, Mary, your father in County Cork always was one to have some put by."

"I'm surprised you'd be mentionin' that, Michael. My father is a farmer, remember? I never heard him talkin' about desertin' his family for a place in the town. My answer is no."

Danny had finished his mush and was staring into the fire. His eye caught the gleam of the musket hanging above the mantel, and he wished he dared ask permission to hunt the next morning. Jacques Le Blanc was leaving for Michilimackinac and it would give Danny an excuse to tell him good-by. But now with his mother upset, he'd have no chance to mention hunting. Dimly he heard his father talking about the advantages of trade. Usually he listened eagerly, hoping his mother might consent to moving inside the fort. But tonight all he could think of was going with Jacques some day to Michilimackinac, the land of the Great Turtle.

"Now, Mary," the O'Hara was saying. "I have a plan if only you'll not be losin' your temper when I tell you."

Mary O'Hara picked up the wooden dishes. "I'm listenin', Michael," she said.

"It's this. And 'twill not be costin' your father a farthing." He leaned forward eagerly. "The French are still doin' most of the tradin' in these parts, but soon the British will be comin' with their trinkets, and then watch. There's not an Englishman or American at Michilimackinac, and that the richest post in the Northwest. Now if we was to get there first, havin' someone like Jacques Le Blanc workin' for us, why come next spring we'd be rich!"

Danny started to speak. Now was his chance to ask permission to go and see Jacques. But his father held up a warning finger. Puzzled, Danny waited.

"And how would we hire a man like that, O'Hara?"

"Aha! That's where me clever mind has been at work. Jacques needs a clerk, a smart young lad who can read and write . . ." But he never finished.

"No you don't, O'Hara." Mary, eyes blazing, put her arms around Danny and held him close. "You'll not be sendin' my only son off among them savages!"

"Now, Mary," the O'Hara argued, "he's almost grown. Look at him settin' there that eager to go. You can't keep him tied down forever!"

Danny tried to squirm loose to say something, but his mother held him fast.

"Not Danny. Why . . ." her eyes filled with tears, "why he's only a baby!" With a wail she turned and ran from the kitchen.

"Can I go, Pa?" Danny found his voice.

His father shook his head. "Not now, lad. Maybe in a

year or two when you're older. Maybe your mother will be after changin' her mind."

Sick at heart, Danny got up from the table and walked slowly to the ladder. As he climbed up to the loft he knew that the evening game with the cannon had only been make-believe. He would never be a real voyageur.

Hunter and Hunted

DANNY O'HARA tossed restlessly on his corn-shuck mattress. Sometime later he had wakened to hear his mother moving downstairs, his father's voice soothing her. Then the lights had gone out and all was quiet. Toward morning he had heard Chief Pontiac grunting in his pen. It reminded Danny of the bear. He had been sure he had seen one. If only he had thought to take a lantern and search for tracks. Wide awake now, Danny, remembering the evening, decided it had been a miserable one.

He didn't suppose he could really blame his mother for not wanting him to leave. He guessed that most mothers were that way. Still, he was no baby! He'd worked as hard as his father, harder maybe. If only there was some way to prove himself. If he had really seen that bear—had shot it, even—then his mother would know that he was grown up. He wished the bear would come back. He would run down, grab the musket, and shoot!

Danny threw back the covers and tiptoed to the window. It had stopped raining and the sky to the east showed false dawn. He craned his neck trying to see where the bear had been. He could make out the bucket still lying there, but that was all. Suddenly Danny was slipping into his clothes. There was only one way to find out the truth. Pulling on his deerskin moccasins, Danny crept carefully down the ladder into the kitchen.

The fire burned low on the hearth, and again Danny saw the gleam of his father's musket. A moment later he was outside, musket in hand, shot pouch and powder horn over his shoulder, searching the ground.

In the soft earth lay the paw marks of the bear. Danny felt his heart beat faster, but he hesitated. Perhaps he should call his father—after all, he had never shot a bear. For a brief moment the musket felt heavy in his hand. He checked the priming. The long muzzle seemed to point toward the retreating paw marks. Danny took a deep breath, squared his shoulders, and started off in pursuit.

The tracks were wider apart now, claws digging deeper where the bear had started his loping run. They twisted around the corner of the fence, then appeared to slow as they reached the path to the fort. For a moment Danny lost them in the tall grass. He circled, half bent over, eyes intent on the ground. There a track, and another. Danny was off again.

He followed them straight to the fort. Outside the walls the bear had stopped to dig around a garbage dump. The sun started its climb above the wooden palisades, and still Danny kept on.

Now they were leading him toward the Indian village, and Danny went more slowly, afraid that the Indian dogs might bark at him. The bear must have been wary too, for now the tracks stayed close to the road curving wide around the round-topped lodges.

He glanced back at the fort. Above the sally port Danny could make out the nodding head of a sentry. The road went close to the tepees now, and still no dogs. Danny stopped and stared at the bark lodges. There was no sign of life. Usually they were filled with gaily dressed braves and their families. Danny shrugged and broke into a dogtrot.

The wet grass ahead was a brown, glistening mat running down to the tall green reeds of the riverbank. Mist, like tattered sails, hung heavily under the distant trees, clinging in pale shreds across the tall spars of the two armed schooners, *Gladwyn* and *Beaver*, anchored in the river.

He realized suddenly that he had lost the trail. This time, circling proved fruitless. If only Jacques were with him, it would be easy to pick up the spoor. Now he would have to go back without the bear and take his punishment. Hopelessly he scanned the surrounding fields. All at once his eye caught a glimpse of the tall pine that marked the path to the cabin of Jacques Le Blanc. Why not go on and see Jacques? And besides, he might pick up the trail again. The thought of finding the bear decided him. He resumed his dogtrot.

His moccasins, sliding now over the grass, made a swishing sound. To Danny the field had become a lake, the swish of his feet the sound of dipping paddles. He was Danny O'Hara, voyageur, winding along the Ottawa River to the north. He began to sing a song of the voyageurs that Jacques had taught him.

From the wilds of the north comes the young voyageur.
With a birchbark canoe well laden with fur,
Gladsome and free, little cares he,
For there's joy in the heart of the young voyageur.

On the "joy in the heart" Danny let his clear young tenor go up and stay a bit. He liked the sound it made echoing against the forest ahead. He stopped singing then, thinking about the north country that Jacques had told him about, and about the Island of the Great Turtle. Michilimackinac was the Ottawa name for it, pronounced "Michilimackinaw." The fort was on the mainland, and called by the same name. Built by the French, it had been the center of the fur trade before the French War. And it would be again, Jacques had said. After all, water was the best and fastest means of transportation, and this was the heart of the Great Lakes. The four lakes, Erie, Huron, Michigan, and Superior, were joined with the waterways to the east by the Straits of Mackinac. Canoes leaving Montreal went up the Ottawa River, portaged to Lake Nipissing and then down the French River to Georgian Bay. From there they entered Lake Huron. The straits were the entrance to Lake Michigan over which they could pass to the west and on down the Mississippi River to other posts. The narrow waterway which connected Lake Huron with Lake Superior at Sault Sainte Marie made it possible to trade far westward.

Danny paused to catch his breath and get his directions. To his right was the tall peeled pine or "lobstick" that Jacques had made to mark his cabin. Ahead the land sloped down into swamp. Good deer country, but too thick to go through. Again Danny checked the priming of his musket. After all, a deer or the bear might wander out of the woods at any moment.

He waited. Nothing moved. Danny looked down at

the long musket and polished the walnut stock with his sleeve. His father would never forgive him if anything happened to the flintlock. The O'Hara had carried it throughout the French War.

Danny glanced at the sun with an uneasy feeling. It was later than he thought, and being this far to the south made him uncomfortable. The Wyandotte village was near, and if a band of hunters came up around the thicket now. . . . He felt his heart beating faster. So far the Indians had been quiet, but not seeing them at the fort had made him wonder what they were up to.

Danny straightened his shoulders. What was there to be afraid of? He was letting the stories his father had told him frighten him. Danny O'Hara, voyageur, shouldn't be afraid. Why, if a hostile Indian came out of the swamp now, he could pick him off easily. He knelt and aimed at the thicket. *"Pow!"* he said. "One down." Pretending to reload, Danny shifted the musket to his shoulder and hurried on toward the peeled pine. Turning sharply at the far end of the swamp, he bent low and entered a thick growth of willows and birch. The path, he knew, should be ahead. Suddenly he stopped and held his breath. Then he was kneeling, his ear pressed to the ground. He heard the sound of moccasined feet on the path directly ahead.

Danny hesitated almost too long before he flung himself face down in the deep grass. Not six feet in front of him a feathered crest flashed by. Another and another. Danny shivered.

Three more steps and he would have run straight into them!

Cautiously, Danny raised his head. They weren't Wyandottes. Their heads were shaven except for scalp-locks! Five, six, seven—Danny was counting—eight, nine. . . . There must be at least fifteen, he decided.

His heart stopped beating. The last Indian slowed, swerved into the grass, and halted. Danny's heart started again, but in great leaping thumps that shook his whole body. He pressed deeper into the grass. The Indian was peering almost directly at him. His face was painted in wide bands of black, and white circles framed his eyes like awful spectacles.

Danny lay motionless, praying that the warrior wouldn't see his red hair. Slowly the Indian raised his bow. Danny tried not to breathe. He could smell the

Indian smell of soot and grease mingling with the odor of wet earth beneath his cheek. The Indian was fitting an arrow to his bow. Danny wanted to cry out, to leap up and run. Instead he closed his eyes and waited for the arrow. The musket lay forgotten at his side.

Red Head

THE ARROW never came. Instead, there was a quick rustle of leaves. Danny forced his eyes open. The Indian had lowered his bow and was springing on down the path. A long belt of wampum flashed purple, flapping against his thighs. Then he was gone.

Danny lay in the grass, feeling the perspiration start down inside his shirt like cold raindrops. After a while he raised himself on his hands and knees, then struggled to his feet. He stood there, listening. All was quiet except for woods noises. A squirrel took up his interrupted chatter high above him. An acorn dropped with a splat.

Danny forced his legs to carry him away from his hiding place. He reached the path, crossed it, and turned back to look at the place where he had been lying. Something moved. The Indian had come back. Danny stood frozen. The leaves parted. Danny leaned against a tree for support and a great sigh burst from his lips. It was only a doe. Nose high, soft eyes bright in the sunlight, the doe stepped forward and began to nibble at the leaves of a young maple.

Now Danny knew. The arrow had been meant for the deer, not for himself, and the doe had disappeared before the Indian could shoot.

The slender animal lowered her head. Ears thrust forward, she looked straight at Danny.

"Thank you, little doe." Danny breathed the words like a prayer. The doe turned and melted into the underbrush. Only then did he realize that he had missed a wonderful shot. Still, the doe had saved his life. Let her go, Danny thought. Then he was staring down at his empty hands. His musket was gone. He must have left it in the woods. Glancing quickly up and down the path, Danny dashed across and back to where he had been lying. There was no sign of the musket. He forced his way through the thick undergrowth.

The sun rose higher. Danny, wet with perspiration, started another circle, coming around through the thick brush in slowly narrowing arcs. Still no musket. Danny sat down and dropped his head in his hands. Shirt torn, blood on his hands and arms from the sharp briers, Danny just managed to keep the tears back. He hadn't shot any game; he hadn't seen Jacques; and now he had lost his father's prized musket. He almost wished the Indian's arrow had found him.

Danny lifted his head. There it was again, a shout coming from the direction of the peeled pine. It must be the voyageurs at Jacques' cabin, loading canoes for the trip. If only he could go with them. Danny jumped to his feet. He would run away. Hadn't his father suggested that he go? Maybe even now, the O'Hara might have convinced his mother. Danny leaped the path and raced for Jacques' cabin. He would send a note back to his parents. His mother, even if she hadn't given her consent, would realize that what he was doing was right. How else could they have enough money to start a store? And his father was on his side. He wouldn't even have to know about the lost musket, and Danny told himself he would bring his father a fine new one from Michilimackinac. The old one had grown rusty, anyway, hanging in the kitchen.

Something flashed ahead of him. It was the river. Danny doubled his speed. In a moment the cabin of Jacques Le Blanc came into view. Danny halted, panting.

The clearing was swarming with Canadians. Eight birch canoes were being loaded. The laughing, singing voyageurs in vivid sashes and shirts, red feathers stuck in woolen hats, moved back and forth between the house and the canoes. Danny watched them wade into the river with the huge bundles and lay them on the poles in the bottoms of the "north canoes." A throng of women and children milled about the clearing, jabbering and shouting at the hurrying men.

Danny waited, trying to catch his breath. He knew that he had to convince Jacques somehow that he must take him—even without the consent of his parents. The door to the cabin opened. Danny saw Jacques coming out with a small voyageur. They seemed to be arguing. Next to the huge bulk of Jacques Le Blanc, the little man looked like a coyote worrying a moose. As they moved closer Danny recognized the little man as Joe Barbeau, called "Joe Loup," the "Wolf." As always, his thin face was twisted into a permanent snarl by the long white scars from forehead to lip which pulled the flesh upward above his sharp teeth. The scars had come from the raking claws of a grizzly bear.

"Oho, Tête-Rouge! Red Head!" Jacques' deep bellow carried easily over the noise.

Danny ran forward. He felt his arms seized in the Canadian's powerful hands and he was lifted off his feet.

"Where have you been? Jacques thought you had forgotten him. But tell me, what are all the scratches and mud on your freckled face?"

Danny's feet touched the ground again and he flexed his arms to bring back the circulation.

"Faith, Jacques, you nearly broke my arms," Danny laughed excitedly. "As for the mud, I was hunting over near the swamp, and I lost Pa's musket, and I saw a band of strange Indians, only they were after a doe instead of me, and. . . ."

"Wait, wait." Jacques threw back his huge head and roared with laughter.

"Sit down, sit down, mon ami, here on this log. You must start from the beginning, but make her short, my little cabbage, or my brigade will not reach the little lake before night."

Danny sat down on a log and tried to think above all the noise. Quickly he told of the evening before, how his father had said that Jacques needed a clerk. With a twinge of guilt Danny carefully left out the part about his mother's refusal.

When he had finished, Jacques looked thoughtful. "And so you wish to become voyageur and make your fortune, eh, Danny?"

"Oh, yes, Jacques!"

"It is not so easy being voyageur. First, you are not

French-Canadian. All voyageurs are, almost. To be born one is a big help. You should have come from a parish near Quebec or Montreal or St. Pierre. You should be born little. Five feet tall—not almost six, as you will be. Your shoulders are wide, that is good; but your legs should be little and skinny. See how my men are big above and little below. They fit the canoe. Then, you do not speak much French. This is bad, but you can sing, which is good. All voyageurs sing."

Jacques paused.

"But you could teach me more French, Jacques," Danny pleaded, "and I could be your clerk. I can read and write."

"A clerk, a *commis*? I don't know. That takes learning. Don't forget, a commis is in charge of a post. Even the *hivernan* works for him. You would have to issue blankets and supplies and keep records. And you are only fourteen."

"I'll be fifteen in January, Jacques."

"So. And you know I need a commis. As you say you can read and write. But you would never make a voyageur. You must be born with a paddle in your hand. And you are too tall."

"But what about you, Jacques? You're big."

"Oho, like a moose, Danny. But big men, they are rare in the Northwest. And then," Jacques' face grew serious, "there is one or two other things, mon ami. First, your papa, he does not come to ask my permission. Why? Second, it is very, very dangerous for Englishman to go to Michilimackinac. The Indians do not like Englishmen here. Do not forget that for one hundred years, they

have French king. Also, many have fought in the war.
They see their families killed by English. They do not
forget these things. There are English troops at the fort,
but too few! And I, Danny, will not be at the fort this
winter. I go to trade along Superior and perhaps even to
the south. Only my old friend, Pierre, my hivernan, with
his Indian wife, Ahwun, and his daughter are watching
over my goods now. Pierre could help you while I am
gone, but it is a big chance you take. If the Ottawa or

Chippewa discover you are not French . . . they might lift your red hair, Danny."

"I'm not afraid, Jacques," Danny pleaded. "Look how I dodged that party of Indians on the trail."

"And lost your musket," Jacques said.

Danny hung his head.

"Look," said Jacques. "You see the man with the grizzly-bear scar?"

Danny looked up. "The man you were talking with?" he asked.

"Oui! He is the one. He wants to be commis. He will be very angry if I say no and give the job to you. He is a bad one, Joe Loup, but a good guide. I wish him to stay as guide, not as commis. He is too much like bad Indian, and so there may be much trouble."

"I'm taller than he is," Danny said. "Feel my muscles, Jacques."

Jacques shook his head. "Perhaps you are taller, Danny, but you have never seen a man of the north fight. Some day when you are big moose like Jacques and are not so skinny, you might beat Joe Loup. Not now. But, my friend, what of your papa and maman? They did not say you could go?"

Danny scuffed his foot. "My pa wants me to, but. . . ."

Jacques said nothing for several minutes. Danny, dreading his answer, waited in agony. What if Jacques refused to take him?

The huge man kept stroking his black beard. Once he took off his red cap and rolled it between his hands. Like a bear with a beehive, Danny thought. Then

Jacques was on his feet. "We leave in one hour. How can you get word to your papa?"

Danny leaped up, his face shining. "You mean I can go, Jacques?"

The Canadian shrugged his shoulders. "I will leave it to you."

"Yii!" Danny let out a yell. "I'll write a note, Jacques. That boy can take it." He pointed to a small urchin.

"And you are willing to dress, think, talk like Canadian?"

"I've always wanted to be like you, Jacques. You can teach me while we're traveling."

Jacques shouted with laughter. "So, I can teach you, eh? And you would be a wild Canadian and live like an Indian?"

Danny's eyes danced. "That I would, Jacques." Watching his huge friend, Danny thought of the time he had first met Jacques. It had been at the fort. Danny had gone down the first day to watch the canoes and had fallen into the river. It had been Jacques who had hauled him out. Since then, the older man had treated him as though he were his own son.

Danny felt Jacques' hand on his shoulder. "Your maman will feel very bad, Danny."

Danny stared at the toes of his moccasins. "I still want to go, Jacques." She would see that he wasn't a baby, he thought.

"Bien, good." He shouted at the small boy, "Bobo!" Motioning for Danny to follow, Jacques started for the cabin.

At the sound of his name the urchin came running.

His only garment was a rough homespun shirt, and as he ran the tails flapped about his bare brown legs. He pointed at Danny's red hair, chanting, "Tête-Rouge, Tête-Rouge," as he ran.

The Young Voyageur

THE CABIN was dark after the brilliance of the sunshine, and Danny closed his eyes for a moment until they were accustomed to the dim light. When he opened them, Jacques had spread a sheet of paper on the rough trestle table and was sharpening a turkey quill.

"First, Danny, comes the 'engagement.' That is what you call a contract. All my men sign them, that is why they are called 'engagés.' It is in French, but it says that you agree to work for one year, will not desert, and will not help rival traders. You want to sign?"

"Sure." Danny took the pen and carefully signed his name at the bottom.

"So, you are hired." Jacques blew on the ink to dry it. "In return you will get clothing for a year, food, and wages. I should pay you like a pork eater, four hundred livres, but instead, as long as we are partners, I will give a share of the furs."

"Are we partners, Jacques? Honest?" Danny said.

"For a year, Danny. We will see after that, how you like the fur trade. Now, here is a piece of paper to write your note. While you are doing this, I will turn you into Canadian."

Danny tried to quiet his growing excitement. He was a voyageur at last. Picking up the pen, he wrote,

Dere Mother and Father—
I am going north. Jac has Hired me. I will be Back next Year. I am sorry to Leave without saying Goodbye. But Jac says Tyme is short. When I come back we will be Rich. Then we can have a Store and you will not be Unhappy.

Y'r obeedyant son
Danny

I saw some Indians with a Wampum Belt.

Danny reread the letter. The ending, where he had said "your obedient son," didn't seem quite right. He wasn't obeying them. Danny took up the pen and crossed out "obedient." Above it he wrote "loving."

Danny looked up to see Jacques stirring something in the pot which hung bubbling in the fireplace.

"I'm ready, Jacques." Danny held out the letter.

Jacques spoke to Bobo in rapid French. Bobo's hand closed tight over the folded note, then he was out the door, the letter clutched against his thin chest.

"Now, Danny," Jacques was grinning. "Lucky thing I have butternut boiling. I was going to dye hunting shirt, but instead I will turn you into Canadian. Come now, off with your clothes and we will see what can be done."

Danny obeyed, wondering. In a moment he stood stripped and shivering in front of the huge Canadian.

Jacques punched Danny's chest with his finger. "You are growing, mon ami, but your ribs stick out. We will fix that. A few weeks in the forests and on the lake, plenty to eat until winter, and you will be a big moose too, like Jacques. When I was your age, I also was scrawny like you. Now, you see this?"

Danny looked at the wooden bowl that Jacques had filled from the slowly boiling kettle. It held a sooty, black liquid and smelled of butternut. He gulped.

Jacques placed the bowl on the table. "Close your eyes, Tête-Rouge, and you shall be redhead no longer." He seized Danny by the scruff of the neck and pressed his head down until his long hair was deep in the black juice. When he let him up at last, Danny felt as though his neck was broken.

"Quick!" Jacques handed him a piece of cloth. "Wipe your face. It will stain bad."

Danny groped for the cloth, rubbed it over his forehead and eyes and then began to dry his hair. "Now what?" Danny grinned up at Jacques, feeling relieved. When he had first seen the liquid, he had been afraid that he might have to drink it.

Jacques stepped to the door and threw the mess into the yard. He came back and dipped the bowl into the kettle again. "More juice," he said. "But this time, no soot in it. This is brown." Jacques dipped a strip of cloth in the amber liquid and handed it to Danny. "Rub this all over. It is butternut. You will be stained brown, like Canadian or Indian—same thing." His white teeth flashed in a smile. "I will rub your back. When you are nice and brown all over like toasted biscuit, you will put on these clothes. They will fit, I think!"

Danny looked at the bundle of clothing that Jacques was taking from a trunk in the corner. "Faith, Jacques. They're just like yours!"

"They are voyageur clothes, Danny. Now rub."

Danny began to smooth the brown-soaked cloth over his face and neck. As he spread the liquid down over his chest and arms, he grinned to see his light skin turning golden. Jacques was dabbing at his shoulders and talking.

"We are going, Tête-Rouge." He glanced at Danny's head. "Oho, Tête-Rouge no longer. Tête-Noire now— black-haired. But as I said, we go to a very wild place. Never forget, mon ami, this place belonged to the French for many years. They do not like the English. So you must be Canadian working for Jacques. This winter perhaps you can learn the Algonquin tongue that is spoken by the tribes to the north. These are the Ottawas and the Ojibways or Chippewa. There are others too, Wyandotte, Miamis, Delaware. As you know, there are many tribes in Canada and in what now belongs to your king. To the east are the fierce Iroquois, friends of the English. Also the Delaware and Mohican. To the north-east, near Quebec, the Algonquin. To the south the Cherokee, Pawnee, the Miami, the Kickapoo. At Michili-mackinac, the Ottawa and Chippewa, like I told you. To the far west, below Lake Superior, the Fox, the Sauk, the Menomini.

"Many tribes fought with the French; some now are after English goods. But you must be careful. Old Pierre will help to keep your secret that you are Englishman. When you arrive, I will take you to see Captain Ether-ington, the English commandant. Also the traders and the Indians. You must learn quickly, mon ami; Jacques can only wait one day to load corn and trade goods, then he will go west. You will be alone with Pierre until I return in the spring. If you are careful and learn well, your share of furs will be good, Danny, and your maman and papa will be proud. If you make a mistake"—Jacques hesitated—"you may never return."

Danny nodded, happily. Even the warning didn't frighten him. The thought of bringing a load of furs to his family made everything else seem unimportant.

"I'm finished, Jacques." Danny dropped the cloth into the kettle. "I'm brown all over now."

"So," Jacques grinned. "And now for your clothes. See, here is a wool cap, red like mine. You cannot wear the feather; that is only for experienced Northmen. Here are two shirts, two pair of leggings of deer skin, a belt, an azion or breechclout, and two pair moccasins. Also blue capote and . . ." he opened the door to the cupboard next to the fireplace. "Here is a sash of scarlet," he chuckled. "You are now a man of the north. All you need is a *sac-à-feu* or tobacco pouch, and a pipe. Every voyageur carries his pipe. It is his watch, his comfort, and sometimes his food."

"His watch?" Danny had pulled on his leggings and was tying the strings to his belt. "How could it be a watch, Jacques?"

"You will see, Danny," Jacques chuckled.

"I will try it, Jacques, but I've never smoked."

"I was joking, Danny. Besides, you are too big now. Once we could have perhaps stunted your growth to make you canoe man." He grinned, "You can forget the pipe, M'sieu Danny."

Danny looked relieved. Slipping on his shirt and moccasins, he adjusted the breechclout. It felt strange to wear leggings that left your thighs bare. He knotted the sash about his waist and faced his friend.

"How do I look, Jacques?"

"Like a voyageur, Danny." He handed him his powder horn and bullet pouch, then stooped to gather up Danny's old clothes. "What about these, mon ami?"

Danny slipped the straps over his shoulder. He settled his red cap over one eye and jerked his thumb toward the fire. "Burn 'em, Jacques," he said.

The huge Canadian shrugged, then tossed the clothes into the flames. Danny didn't even glance at the smoking cloth. He picked up his extra clothes and swaggered out the door in an exact imitation of Jacques Le Blanc.

Michilimackinac

D ANNY STOOD impatiently on the rough pier at the river's edge and counted the canoes. There were seven "north canoes" and one Indian. The north canoes were twenty-five feet long, able to hold a crew of eight and three thousand pounds, yet so light that two men could carry them easily on their shoulders. Almost dancing with excitement, Danny saw Jacques moving about the clearing, shouting orders. His swarthy engagés eyed Danny with good-natured scorn. They had seen pork eaters before, but this time their *bourgeois* had said the boy would be their commis. Danny failed to catch the sly winks and whispers that passed among the men. Even Joe Loup's silent rage at being cheated out of the job which he felt should have been his passed unnoticed as Danny watched the final "piece" laid carefully on the long poles in the last canoe.

The wonderful canoes, Danny thought. Just what he had dreamed of. He knew how they were made; Jacques had told him. The bark from a single white birch was sewn into strips with red spruce root called *wattape*. This was stretched over a skeleton frame of thin white-cedar boards. Twenty-five feet for the north canoes, forty for the huge "Montreal canoes," and fifteen for the light or Indian canoe such as he and Jacques were to use. Pointed at both ends, four to six feet wide at the center, the bark was lashed to the gunwales with wattape. Narrow bars of thwarts across the top held the canoe in shape while four-inch boards, suspended several inches below the gunwales, served as seats.

Danny couldn't help but marvel at the colorful designs painted on the bows. There were Indian heads, bears, flags, painted in bright colors. The small canoe had green and yellow stripes along the gunwale with a running deer in red on the bow. The paddles were red also, with black and green designs. Danny saw that the six middlemen sat in the three middle seats and carried two-foot paddles. The steersman and bowsman carried longer, wider ones. The other equipment included a sponge for bailing, a rope or cordelle for towing, and an oilcloth. The oilcloth was for covering the cargo, or it could be used for a sail when the wind was right.

"*Alerte, alerte.*" A cry went up from the men. Danny turned to see the voyageurs seizing paddles and running toward the loaded canoes. Jacques was coming from the cabin, carrying a hide-covered chest on his shoulder.

A great babble of voices rose from the women and children on the bank. Danny had to shout to make himself heard over the din.

"Jacques," he shouted. "Over here!"

The big man pushed his way through the crowd. "We go, Danny," he bellowed in French.

Danny grinned. How lucky he had been, he thought, to have lived next to French-Canadian farmers. By the time they reached the fort, he would be speaking French like a native.

"Into the canoe, Commis. We will follow the brigade. I think it best that you learn to paddle with Jacques, no?"

"Sure, Jacques," Danny answered. He stepped carefully into the center of the light craft. It moved beneath him like a spirited horse. He sat down quickly in the bow, seized his paddle, and glanced back over his shoulder.

The big man swung the trunk lightly into the canoe, then with the ease of a man half his size, the bearded Canadian leaped into the stern and gave a mighty shove. The canoe leaped away from the bank. They were off!

Ahead of him Danny saw the brigade fanning out on the river. Far ahead, the steersman of the lead canoe shouted the first verse of a song. Instantly, a roar of sound flooded the river as the voyageurs roared the chorus. Paddles flashed red, forty strokes to the minute.

They had covered barely two canoe lengths before Danny forgot the brigade and the river and the song. He was trying desperately to keep his paddle from being wrenched out of his hands as Jacques drove the canoe forward. Dip, dip. Danny's shoulder began to ache. He bit his lips. At his back he heard Jacques' voice, calm in the excitement, urging him on, telling him his mistakes —insistent, driving. Danny found himself gasping for breath.

The song ended.

"*Allumez.*" A cry went up from the steersman. Danny felt the canoe drift. He looked up. The voyageurs were resting their dripping paddles across the thwarts.

"Rest, Danny." Jacques' voice was at his back again. "You see now the meaning of the pipe."

Danny turned his head and managed a grin.

"The pipe," Jacques continued, "she is our watch. When the foreman calls 'Allumez,' we rest. We take the pipe from our beaded sac-à-feu—so—and smoke. It is the way we measure our rests on portage when we carry our canoes, and on the water. You see, Danny?"

"I see, Jacques, but I don't think I need a pipe to tell me when I need a rest." Danny pulled off his wool cap and mopped his forehead.

"You weary so soon?" Jacques' eyes twinkled. "That is why we took the small canoe. You are not voyageur yet. If you were in a north canoe, my men would make your life so miserable, that you would wish to be back on the farm again."

"No I wouldn't," Danny said stubbornly.

"Perhaps these would help." Jacques took two pieces of leather from his sash and handed them forward to Danny. "Tie them on your hands, mon ami. It will save the blisters."

"Thanks, Jacques." Danny took the two strips of doeskin and wrapped them around his reddened palms.

"We go! *Allons!*" Danny felt the canoe leap forward. Ahead the vermilion paddles were flashing. Water from the sterns began spreading out like snowy furrows on a green field. Detroit was slipping away. Danny dipped his paddle.

Another pipe, and another. Danny began to dread the cry of "Allumez." The rest only seemed to make the renewed paddling harder.

It wasn't until the sun finally dropped behind the for-

Danny seized his paddle and glanced over his shoulder

est wall that the exhausted Danny saw the canoes turn shoreward.

For the last hour, Danny had been thinking of nothing but camp. To stretch his legs and put down the terrible paddle—these two thoughts were all that kept him going. But now, as the canoes glided toward shore, Danny was sure that his legs would never support him. The other voyageurs were springing out of their canoes into the shallow water. Danny summoned his last bit of strength. The canoe touched the bank. He tried to stand, but his legs refused to support him. They were like sticks, he thought, dead sticks that didn't belong to him. He grasped the gunwales. Jacques was already out of the canoe. Danny felt a hand at his belt. The next moment he was lifted like a sack of peas and dropped on the shore.

Danny struggled up on shaking legs. A great shout of laughter rose from the throats of the voyageurs. He stood there, swaying, feeling the great knots of pain rising in his calves.

"How goes it, Pork Eater?"

Danny heard the shout. Dimly he saw Joe Loup with two ninety-pound pieces on his back. He was wading ashore as easily as if they were empty sacks.

Danny flushed angrily, driving himself toward the beached canoe. He bent over and his hand closed on the ropes that held the small tent. He lifted it to his shoulder and started haltingly for the clearing. One step after another, eyes stinging with sweat, he reached the clearing at last and dumped the tent onto the ground. Danny straightened and turned back for the second trip. The pain in his legs was lessening, but another pain was taking its place. Jacques Le Blanc, his friend, was standing with the others and he too was laughing. Danny made his way back to the canoe. Somehow he managed to lift a single piece but only as high as his waist. His feet sank deep into the spongy riverbank as he tried to get the pack onto his shoulder. He went down on one knee. Then someone was at his side. The pack slid easily up onto his back and Jacques' voice was in his ear.

"You are doing fine, mon ami. Do not let the laughter give you pain. It is always so with a new man."

New strength seemed to come into Danny then. He got to his feet and walked to the clearing without faltering. He even helped Jacques carry the canoe ashore and turn it over, bottom up, on the ground.

Danny straightened his aching shoulders. "What next, Jacques?" he said, as he sat down heavily on the grass.

Jacques winked. "Next we pitch the tent and then— *souper!*"

The following two hours were a blur to Danny. He remembered helping with the tent and squatting just outside, half asleep, while someone urged him to eat. Then he was stretched out on a bed of hemlock branches, wrapped in his blanket. He awakened sometime later to the sound of singing. At first he thought he was in his bed in the loft. Danny sat up. His head touched canvas. A sudden clanging brought him crawling to the tent door. He lifted the flap and looked out.

The clearing was filled with moving shadows. Huge in the light of the roaring fire, they slid across the ground like creeping giants.

Shivering, Danny crept closer. A sack had been placed at each end of the clearing. On the sacks sat two voyageurs; one a grizzled veteran named Henri, the other a boy. Firelight shone on their faces and on their flashing spoons as they beat a strange rhythm on the kettles under their arms. Around them in a swaying circle stamped the voyageurs.

The dancers slowed and stopped. The old man began to sing. Danny tried to make out the French words. He was singing something about going north in a canoe. The old man stopped singing and the boy answered him. "We are good good fellows," he sang. "We are unafraid." Again the beat of the spoons on iron while the voyageurs took up their dance, roaring the refrain.

The dancers stopped. "Good-by, Mother and Father," sang the boy; "good-by, brother. You will soon see your son again."

The dance went on, but Danny had crawled back inside his blankets. Voyageurs don't cry, he told himself over and over, but the homesickness welled up in him. He buried his head in his blanket. The noise of the singers drowned his sobbing. He slept at last, and dreamed wild dreams full of black shadows.

The stars faded. A chill wind came with the gray light filtering down through tossing branches. Danny opened his eyes. He was looking up into the sky. Where was the tent? Heart pounding, he threw off his blanket and sat upright.

A loud laugh brought him scrambling to his feet. Two voyageurs, carrying his rolled tent between them, were prancing toward the already loaded canoes. Cheeks burning, Danny snatched up his blanket and began to make it into a clumsy bundle. By the time he had folded the heavy blankets and tightened his sash and leggings, the stiffness in his body was leaving; but the ache in his muscles made him want to groan with pain.

He started for the canoe, each step a misery. Tomorrow morning, he told himself angrily, he would be the first one awake. And he would take down his own tent, too. He reached the bank and flung his blanket into the bow of Jacques' canoe. At least they wouldn't have to wait for him. Intent on straightening the tent that the two voyageurs had tossed carelessly into the canoe, Danny failed to notice that the others had gone back to the clearing. He finished tying down the tent and threw one leg over the gunwale.

"Hurry, Commis. Perhaps you can catch breakfast on the river!"

Danny turned. Old Henri was pointing at him, laughing. The men were in a circle around the campfire. They held smoking bowls of food, and they too were laughing at him.

Danny hesitated, shamefaced. It was his hunger that finally drove him back to the campfire.

Jacques was waiting as he came up. He handed Danny a bowl and spoon. "Good morning, Danny," Jacques boomed. "Did you think the tent had flown?"

The men, their mouths full of pork, peas, and biscuits, nudged each other, chuckling.

Danny dug his spoon into the hot food. He ate four spoonfuls in rapid succession. While he ate, he was thinking what to say in reply. The voyageurs were watching him. He decided to bluff it through. "I wasn't surprised," he said loudly in his best French. "The wind you made singing last night was enough to blow any tent away. That is, if you call that *singing*," he grinned.

"Aha! Henri," someone called. "He calls your singing wind."

Catcalls and laughter followed.

"So?" Old Henri came over and stood in front of Danny. "And perhaps you can sing better, no?"

Danny felt the crowd grow quiet. It's now or never, he thought. He put the bowl on the ground. "Sure I can," he said.

A hand seized his collar and Joe Loup thrust his scarred face close to Danny's. "You talk big. Perhaps you fight big, too?"

Old Henri stepped in. "Let him sing, Joe Loup."

"Let him sing," said the others.

Joe Loup slunk back, but his face wore a look of hatred that Danny would never forget.

Danny cleared his throat. "From the wilds of the north," he began. His voice gained strength. He was singing in French and singing with all he had, forgetting the men around him. When he reached the last line, ". . . there is joy in the heart," Danny held the word "heart," letting his voice soar straight up against the tall pines.

Then it was over—or was it? Old Henri had picked up the verse and was singing at the top of his voice. Another and another joined in. At his side, Jacques' rolling bass caught up the tune.

Danny sang four verses, the men joining in at the

chorus. When he finished he didn't need Jacques' rib-bursting thump on his back to know that he had made up for his mistakes of the morning. A half hour later, it was a happier Danny who sat at the bow of Jacques' canoe.

Another day came and went. His hands still pained fiercely and his shoulder muscles burned, but that night as he lay in his blanket he began to feel a part of the camp. The chirping crickets, the hoarse croaking of frogs blurred against the backdrop of night in what seemed a friendly chorus. When morning came, he was awake before the others. This time, to the huge delight of the voyageurs, it was Jacques who looked up at the open sky.

Up and away. The brigade bobbed in the short choppy waves of Lake St. Clair. By noon the forest along the bank closed in and the canoes struck the surging current of the river again.

The third day, Danny noticed that the paddling was easier. His palms, growing hard under the deerskin, held the paddle lightly, riding with the sweep instead of fighting the current.

With the blue horizon of Lake Huron around them, Jacques' voice at his back was less urgent. Instead it seemed to reflect some of the sparkle of the water as he paused in a song to tease or scold Danny, repeating French words and waiting for Danny's answer.

Learning fast, his glib Irish tongue pouncing on the new phrases, Danny repeated them after Jacques, then said them over and over at night remembering them.

The days slipped away like water from the bow of the lead canoe. The tall, shaggy fir trees along the western shore seemed almost to be moving by themselves. Forty strokes to the minute, pause for the *"pipe,"* then on again. At last Bois Blanc, the island of the White Forest, thrust its birch-crowned head against the clear sky. Then, ahead, something flat on the horizon. It was only a blur of gray but it brought a shout from Jacques. Danny shading his eyes, let out an answering whoop. Michilimackinac, the Island of the Great Turtle, lay on the horizon.

Like one, the eight canoes swung to the left.

"We are almost to the fort, Danny," Jacques said. "It is to our left on the mainland there. Only Chippewa live on the island. Chippewa means 'puckered.' They are called this because of the style of their moccasins. You will see them soon, no doubt."

Danny nodded happily, little dreaming what the word Chippewa would mean to him in the coming weeks. Suddenly he grinned. Jacques had spoken in French, and he had understood every word.

Singing lustily, the canoemen doubled their speed, racing for the sandy beach, each trying to see who would be first to reach the shore. Danny and Jacques bent their backs, driving their canoes over the water at top speed. The shore came closer. Danny could see the stony bottom far below. He dipped his paddle hard and paused to look again. They were almost to the beach. With a shout, Danny leaped over the side. Jacques drove his paddle into the water with a final shove just as Danny's red-capped head disappeared under the waves.

Danny felt the water close over his head. He struggled upward, fighting for air. His feet touched gravel. Danny rose to the surface, gasped, choked, and gained his footing. Ahead of him he saw Jacques doubled up with laughter. Danny struggled toward shore. Who would have thought the water could be so clear! The bottom had looked to be only a few feet away.

Then Jacques was pounding him on the back.

"Now you are baptized, Danny; you are true Northman," Jacques roared.

Danny wiped the water from his face and looked down at his dripping clothes. "This lake fools you," he said.

"But we won the race, Danny. We won the race," Jacques said. "Now, here is your new home. How do you think it will be for a winter, eh, Commis?"

Danny looked around him. Indian canoes lined the shores. Canadians, some with Indian wives, shouted a welcome to the new arrivals.

Danny, lifting packs onto the beach, saw a small band of wooden-faced Indians watching them. Suddenly he felt a stab of fear. These looked like the band he had seen running on the path near Detroit. He glanced at their moccasins. The toes were puckered. Chippewa—the runners had been Chippewa. Danny looked for Jacques. He wanted to tell him of his discovery, but the crowd was growing larger. Danny went back to his work. He would have to tell Jacques later.

The beach was swarming now with laughing, shouting voyageurs. Indian women, their deerskin dresses loaded with beads and quills, stood shyly next to their naked children or laughed shrilly at the antics of the bearded engagés. The children, their hair thick with vermilion, scuttled back and forth, shrieking, tugging, begging for trinkets.

"Look, Danny." Jacques pointed to a long low shed. "Our warehouse," he said, and laughed like a child with a new trinket.

Then Jacques was unlocking the door. Danny stepped in behind him. The chinked log walls at the back were bare except for a long bunk. A great rough table stood in the center of the room, surrounded by kegs. At the front was a crude counter, and shelves ran along the side wall. On the other wall stood the stone fireplace. The room smelled of hides.

Late that afternoon, after the bundles from the canoes had been stacked inside, Danny went with Jacques on a tour of the fort. He met countless settlers, traders, and Indians, even Captain Etherington, the English commandant.

As Danny walked back to the post, the names of those he had met kept whirling about in his mind. He wondered how he could possibly remember them all. He had not met Pierre. The winterer who was to help him had not yet returned from the island where he had gone with his wife and daughter after fish. He hoped the old man would return before Jacques left.

Souper was late. Tired of their usual diet of peas and pork, the men had taken time to catch whitefish for their meal. Now they lounged on bundles around the fire in the main room of the store while the air grew blue with the smoke of many pipes.

Danny sat fighting sleep. He kept hoping that Old Pierre would come in, but there had been no sign of him as yet.

At last Danny excused himself. He had work to do,

getting his papers in order for the morrow. If there were any questions to ask, he would have to think of them now, for Jacques was leaving as soon as they could take on more supplies. No chance then to depend on Jacques. He, Danny O'Hara, was the commis. The word made him puff out his chest a little. It would be harder with Jacques gone, but the men now seemed to accept him as one of them. All but Joe Loup!

Danny longed for sleep, but he had work to do. He took up a candle and made his way to his room in the rear. Wearily he spread his blankets in his bunk.

He had just opened the chest to look at his new journal and was laying out quills and ink for the morrow when he heard a thud of feet in the front room, followed by Jacques' bellow of rage.

Danny dropped the lid of the trunk and ran to the door. Joe Loup stood at the foot of the table. He kept dabbing at his twisted mouth with one hand. A thin trickle of blood stained his chin, and to Danny he looked like a weasel cleaning himself after a stolen meal of chicken.

"I told you once, Joe!" Jacques thundered. "Forget about M'sieu Danny. *He* is my commis, not you. And he is to remain Canadian. If I hear you call him *Anglais* in front of the Chippewa again, I will break you into little pieces!"

Joe Loup backed off snarling something, his bared teeth sharp, curved like the teeth of an Indian dog.

Jacques' hand shot out, but the small man was quicker. He whirled and ran out into the darkness.

"That is a warning to you all!" Jacques faced the

others. "If anyone say Anglais again, he will be sent away! Henri, you will take Joe's place at the bow of the lead canoe. We leave without Joe Loup!"

The men said nothing. Jacques started for the back room; then he saw Danny.

"Ah," he said. "You heard, Danny? It was nothing. We all understand now." He glanced back at the men who sat watching him. No one spoke. "All right, by gar!" Jacques pushed Danny into the back room.

"Danny," he said, "it does not matter this time, what Joe said. But we must be careful. Next time I see Joe, I throw him into the lake. He cannot swim a stroke! Then it will be the end of Joe Loup!" Jacques chuckled. "Now forget your books; it is too late. Go to sleep, boy, dream of how you will return to Detroit a rich trader, eh? You can buy Maman a fine silk dress."

Danny let himself be pushed toward the bunk. He wished he were going with Jacques instead of staying in this strange place alone, but he managed a grin. "All right, Jacques. I'll see you in the morning."

"That is good, Commis. Jacques will return with the wild geese in the spring, as soon as the ice leaves the rivers. Pierre will be here in the morning, I am sure. Until then, close your door and sleep. My men grow noisy but soon they too will sleep like little babies."

"Good night, Jacques."

"Good night, Danny. May le bon Dieu keep you safe."

Danny removed his moccasins. Then, without bothering to undress, he blew out the candle and climbed into his bunk. The warm blanket settled across his chest like a soft hand. He wondered what his mother was doing.

Englishman

THE LAST of the canoes passed out of sight an hour after dawn. Danny walked slowly back up the path to the fort. The store was empty. Danny sat down on a pile of skins and gazed at the list of duties that Jacques had given him, but the words seemed meaningless. He gave up and moved over to the window. The canoes were on their way west. Danny thought of the two empty places left in them. One had been his and the other Joe Loup's. He wished that Joe Loup had not stayed behind. Jacques had refused to hire him back again, and Joe had gone away with a band of Indians. He hoped Joe would stay away, but why worry? Didn't Fort Michilimackinac belong to the king? Captain Etherington and Lieutenant Leslie and the garrison of Royal Americans were in command—he had seen them yesterday—and the captain was sure that there would be no more Indian trouble.

Well, thought Danny, he would let things come as they would. No use in jumping at shadows. He turned away from the windows and reached for the list on the counter. Someone was standing in the doorway. Danny looked up, startled.

"Bon jour. Good day, M'sieu Daniel."

"M'sieu." Danny recovered from his momentary fright,

answered in the French patois of the *habitant* or settler. "What is it you wish?"

The little man came forward. He wore a blue capote, covered with patches, leggings that had once been scarlet, patched at the knees with deerskin, and a huge cap of wolf fur. It was the cap that interested Danny. The long wolf hairs hanging down around the old man's head blended with his thick grizzled hair and beard so closely that it was hard to decide which was the cap. Even his nose seemed to be trying to find an opening in the underbrush. It curved down over the bristling mustaches, a signpost pointing a way for the snapping black eyes to follow. The eyes gazed steadily at Danny, then almost disappeared in what Danny felt must be a smile.

"Ah, my friend," the old man bowed slightly, "it is I who have something for you—a bit of news." His voice was suprisingly deep for such a small man.

Sitting down on the keg, the old man began to shred the tobacco into his pipe.

Suddenly Danny realized who his visitor was—it must be Old Pierre, the winterer.

Danny leaned his elbows on the counter and waited. When Pierre had lighted his pipe, he spoke.

"I am sorry," the old man said, "that I missed our good friend, Jacques. Others have told me that you are the new commis and that I am to assist you."

"I am grateful, M'sieu Pierre."

"So, you remember my name." The old man looked pleased. "I came quickly when I learned that you were here and alone. I have news which my wife, Ahwun, has told me."

"And what is the news?"

"That you are an Englishman!" The old man was watching him closely.

"Is that all?" Danny scowled. What was the old man trying to say?

Pierre replaced his pipe and studied the bales piled about the room.

Danny waited for him to speak. He was beginning to feel uneasy.

"There is more." Pierre's eyes fastened on Danny again. "It is of no matter to me. Jacques and I are friends for many years. If he wishes to have an English commis,

it is not my affair. But there are others who are not happy that the Englishman has come into our trading grounds."

"But this fort belongs to the king. Why shouldn't we come?" Danny was growing impatient. Why didn't the old man tell what he had come to tell, instead of just sitting and smoking?

Old Pierre ignored the question; taking his pipe again from his mouth, he jabbed the stem toward Danny's chest. "Do you speak the Algonquin tongue?"

"Very little. Jacques taught me a few words, but that is all." Danny moved back from the pointing pipestem.

"And do you know who lives on the Island of the Great Turtle?"

"Yes. Chippewa."

"They are coming to see you. All of them!" The old man bent closer, waiting for Danny to speak.

Danny's eyes flew wide. "Coming to see me?" A knot was forming in his stomach, and his palms felt damp. "Why should they do that?"

Pierre shrugged his shoulders. "Who knows? They have learned from someone that you are an Englishman and they have sent word that you are to meet them outside the fort. It is not unusual for them to do this when a new trader comes. The Chippewa, and the Ottawa as well, make it a practice. They come with their chiefs to welcome the new trader with gifts for which, of course, they expect a larger one. I see that you have enough goods to make them a present."

Danny wondered bitterly why Jacques hadn't thought to warn him. He tried to keep his voice calm as he spoke. "Who told them I was English?"

Pierre shrugged his shoulders.

"Was it Joe Loup?"

Pierre grinned. "You are no fool, M'sieu. Joe Loup was a very angry man."

Thoroughly frightened now, Danny moved back against the wall. "When are they coming?" he asked.

"Today."

"Today!" Danny stared at the old man, openmouthed. "But," he stammered, "I can't even understand their language!"

"That is why I hurried," Pierre said.

Danny felt his courage coming back. To face the Chippewa alone. . . . He let out a sigh of relief. "And you will stay with me, Pierre?"

The old man nodded and smiled. "Don't be ashamed of your fear, Danny. You are young and do not understand the ways of the Indian as yet. I am old, and my wife is a Chippewa. Her full name is Ahwun Ogomahqua, Lady of the Mist. I will help you, and I will teach you the language of the Chippewa as well."

Danny's eyes shone with gratitude. "We will be friends, Pierre?" He held out his hand.

The old man stood up quickly and seized Danny's hand in a powerful grip. "Friends," he said. "Now, let us choose a present for the chiefs."

Danny knelt beside him and together they untied a bundle of trade goods. Soon a great heap of things lay spread out on the pine-plank floor.

"Ah, this will do nicely. So!" Pierre selected a roll of gold braid, two stroud blankets, and several pots of vermilion.

Pierre appeared satisfied.

Danny wondered if he should offer the old man some-thing. There was a bundle of capotes in a corner. Danny pulled it into the light. The old man was watching him silently, puffing again on his pipe. Danny untied the leather and took a coat from the pile. It was a small size, as were most of the blue-hooded coats. From the corner of his eye he saw Pierre take his pipe from his mouth and bend closer. His dark eyes gleamed through his tangle of eyebrow and fur cap.

Danny held the coat up and smoothed the wrinkles from the heavy wool. Then he handed it to Pierre. "For you, M'sieu."

The Canadian started back, trying to hide the pleasure on his wrinkled face. "Ah, but no, M'sieu Daniel. I can-not accept such a costly present."

"Please, Pierre," Danny urged. "Jacques would be angry if you refused. It is only to pay you for acting as my interpreter."

Pierre's shoulders lifted almost to his ears in a shrug. "If you insist, M'sieu." He took the hooded coat, hefted it, then stroked the wool with a gnarled hand. Bowing and smiling, he turned to go. "Until this afternoon, Danny," he said. Pierre bowed again and shuffled out the door.

Back at the counter, Danny picked up the braid and blankets that Pierre had chosen. Wouldn't the Chip-pewa be pleased when they saw the flash of the gold on the braid! Danny put the goods on the counter. And how excited the old Canadian had been with his new coat.

Danny looked down at his own clothes. They were

stained with grease and soot. If he was to be host to the Chippewa, he should look his best. Somewhere he had seen a mirror. Danny began rummaging through the pack that Pierre had opened. There it was, a cheap trade mirror. Danny moved to the window and held up the glass. The face that stared back at him seemed strange. Danny looked closer. He could stand a bath, or at least wash his face. Was that a line of whiskers around his mouth? Danny thrust out his upper lip and peered into the wavy reflection. Sure enough, there was a line of golden fuzz on his upper lip. Danny put down the mirror and grinned. He would wash, put on a new coat, shirt, and leggings. He might even stick an ostrich feather in his cap as he had seen the voyageurs do. And then— Danny reached for his hunting knife—he would have his first shave!

Pulling off his soiled garments, Danny O'Hara suddenly began to feel very important.

Sawaquot

D ANNY, IN blue-and-white checked shirt, scarlet
leggings, and sash, stood at the door watching
for Pierre to return. He had thrust an ostrich
feather in his cap and he had only two small nicks on his
chin to show where his knife had slipped. His black-dyed
hair hung to his shoulders and his blue eyes were sparkling with excitement. As Pierre came up, Danny raised
his hand in greeting. In spite of the warm sun, the old
man wore his new coat proudly and he had exchanged
his fur hat for a scarlet kerchief.

"The Chippewa have been sighted," Pierre said. "They
will be here soon. We must hurry."

Danny felt the hair on his scalp prickle. In the excitement of wearing new clothes, he had almost forgotten
the reason for the visit of the chiefs.

"Where do we meet them, Pierre?" Danny had trouble
keeping his knees from shaking.

"Come, I will take you." The old man calmly shoul-
dered the trade goods and started off. Danny had no
choice but to follow. He managed to lock the door and
hurried after Pierre.

As they walked, Danny kept trying to think what his
father would do in a situation like this. The O'Hara never
seemed to be at a loss, no matter how many people were

around. Still, these weren't settlers coming; they were Indians. Danny wished fervently for the comforting bulk of Jacques Le Blanc.

Pierre said, "I have hopes, Danny, that the chief who leads them will be Sawaquot. His name in the Algonquin tongue means 'Fork-in-the-Tree.'"

"Is he a friendly chief?" Danny asked hopefully.

"He likes the English," Pierre answered. "Your Sir William Johnson, who defeated us at Niagara, gave Sawaquot a medal for loyalty. Sawaquot is also my wife's brother."

Danny felt his courage mounting.

Pierre continued. "Sawaquot is the only sachem of this tribe who thinks the English king is his father. The others remember the war." He paused.

"I hope Sawaquot will lead them," said Danny.

"We will see, M'sieu. The meeting will be outside the fort. Since the house of the commandant of the English is now filled with soldiers, there is no other place to meet. See, we are at the gates. The Chippewa will land there." Pierre pointed toward where Danny had landed only the day before.

As Pierre talked on, Danny listened eagerly, hoping to learn as much as he could before the Indians arrived.

Pierre was still talking when they reached the gates. There he stopped and spread the two blankets on the ground. After he had piled the paint pots and braid on top, he seated himself with his back to the fort and motioned for Danny to do the same.

"Now, Daniel, you must listen carefully to what they

say, and I will translate. They will pass the pipe, from which you must take three puffs, then pass it on."

A pipe, thought Danny! He had never tasted tobacco in his entire life!

"When the smoke is finished," continued Pierre, "you must stand and make a speech in answer."

"A speech! Me make a speech!" Danny looked at Pierre in dismay.

"Of course. It will be easy. Just tell them that you are glad to be among the brave Chippewa and that you will be happy to trade with them. Then you will pass out the presents. Simple, no?"

Danny sat stunned. Simple to make a speech in front of a whole tribe of Indians? He wiped his forehead with the back of his hand.

"Look." Pierre pointed toward the shimmering lake. "Here they come. Remember what I have told you, and remember also that Jacques is depending on you."

Danny watched the long parade of canoes heading for the shore. He ran his fingers nervously through his hair. A lot of good the dye had done, he thought. Everyone seemed to know he was English. Then, before he could think any more, the canoes were being pulled up onto the sand. A procession of warriors started toward them. Danny groaned aloud. Nearly a hundred braves were in the procession. Pierre glanced at him in warning. On came the Chippewa. Each painted brave carried a tomahawk in one hand and a scalping knife in the other. Silently, looking straight ahead, the Indians spread out into a wide circle; then at a sign from their leader, they seated themselves on the ground.

Danny gazed about him in near panic, wanting desperately to get up and run. Never before had he seen so many Indians. Most of them were naked to the waist. A few had blankets thrown over their shoulders, and all were gaudily painted with charcoal and vermilion. White patterns of clay snaked about their chests and arms, while the hawk and eagle feathers that were thrust through their scalp locks and even through their noses bobbed and swayed in the soft breeze from the lake.

Danny tore his eyes away and looked at Pierre. He was sitting cross-legged, staring ahead of him with such an expression of boredom that Danny felt his spirits rise a little. There was a sudden movement among the circle. Danny jumped at the sound of a deep voice speaking in a strange guttural. It was a tall Indian of about fifty. His powerful figure was straight, and he spoke with great dignity. Danny prayed that it was Fork-in-the-Tree.

Pierre was listening carefully, his eyes on the chief. The tall Indian ceased speaking. Pierre answered. Danny caught a word here and there—"Howh," which meant "yes"; "Meno," which meant "good."

Pierre stopped speaking and turned to Danny. "Sawaquot says the Englishman must be brave to come alone into the country that holds so many of his enemies. I have answered yes, that you are a good friend of the Chippewa. Now we will smoke."

So it was Fork-in-the-Tree! Danny breathed easier.

Sawaquot now seated himself, and Danny saw the warriors take long pipes from beneath their blankets and fill them. Soon the blue smoke began rising from their calumets in slow spirals. Danny told himself that he must try not to choke when the time came for him to smoke. He let his eyes move over the silent circle, trying to imitate Pierre's manner.

The braves wore all kinds of trinkets. Some had hawk's bells hanging from their leggings; others wore shell earrings dangling over parts of uniforms. Gold buttons gleamed here and there, while some had shining gorgets hanging about their copper-colored throats. Danny could make out the letters on them, "G.R.," George Rex, parts of British officers' uniforms. Danny wondered where they had gotten them. Then he knew, and the thought made his scalp prickle—these were braves who had fought for the French in the French War. Those gorgets were from dead British officers.

The pipes were finished. Danny saw Fork-in-the-Tree rise and take a message belt of wampum in one hand. Danny tried desperately to quiet his trembling legs and arms. After all, there was a garrison at his back. He wondered if the soldiers or the captain were watching him from the fort, but he didn't dare turn to look. Pierre's elbow was in his ribs.

"Listen now, and do not let them know you are afraid or all is lost."

Danny clenched his hands. Pierre began to translate.

"Englishman!" Sawaquot was speaking. "It is to you I speak and I demand your attention. Englishman, you know that the French king has been the Chippewa's father and we once promised to be his children forever. This promise we kept until you made war upon him and drove him away. So now, while the English tell us that we are the children of the English king, we have received very few presents and we are not pleased. We know that you took possession of Canada while our French father was sleeping and that he has not returned. But still you do not treat the Chippewa as well as he did." He paused, fingering his wampum. There were cries of "Mah-nah-dud!" from the warriors and Danny felt as though a cold wind was ruffling the hairs on his neck. Pierre was translating.

"The others say it is bad, bad."

"Englishman." Fork-in-the-Tree was speaking again. "You have known that the French king was our father, and employed our young men to make war on your nation. Many of them were killed, and there has been much wailing in the lodges of my people. It is our custom, upon the death of our young men, to pay back our enemies until the spirits of the slain are satisfied. Englishman, this is done in two ways. First, by spilling the blood of our enemies who have done this thing. The second way is by covering the bodies of the slain so that they are satisfied. This is done by making presents.

"Englishman, your king has sent us a few presents, and we are not at war with him. Treaties also have been signed, so now we shall serve our father, the English king. You, Englishman, have come among us without weapons and with our friends, the Canadians. Do not expect us to harm you. You shall be as our brother, Englishman, without fear, for the Chippewa will let you sleep in peace. As a token of this, we give you this pipe to smoke."

A younger brave stepped forward and handed a long pipe to Danny. He put it to his lips and drew in smoke, cautiously. It was strangely sweet. Danny puffed twice more, then handed it to Pierre, who puffed three times, then started it around the circle. Danny ran his tongue over his lips. The smoke had puckered his tongue and his mouth was dust-dry.

"Now you must answer him." Pierre's whisper was urgent.

Danny forced himself to his feet. His legs seemed as though they belonged to someone else. Unconsciously, he took his father's favorite stance—legs apart, one hand thrust in his belt, the other behind him, feeling one hundred pairs of black eyes crawling over him like black leeches before fastening themselves to his face. He managed to look above their heads and opened his mouth to speak. "Brothers." The French words came hard.

"Louder!" hissed Pierre.

"Brothers!" Danny almost shouted the word. "I have come to trade with you for my friend Jacques Le Blanc, who has taken his canoes to the West. Pierre has told me of your bravery and"—Danny paused—"and I am glad to have come to trade among you." Danny stole a glance at Pierre. The old man looked up at him and winked one eye solemnly. When Danny spoke again, his voice was almost confident.

"Brothers, you are great warriors. The English king, your father, is proud that you are now his children. That is why our canoes are laden with presents. Today I have brought only small gifts for your great chief, Sawaquot, and your warriors, but there are many fine things waiting in our storehouse. May we live together in peace." Danny sat down. Perspiration poured down his face, but the crushing weight was gone from his chest. Now, if only the Chippewa liked what he had said. Pierre was translating; Danny looked around hoping to read something in the painted faces about him.

Pierre was finished. Instantly there was a chorus of "Howh, howh!" The old man turned and smiled.

"They like it, Daniel; they like it."

Danny couldn't help but grin. He looked at the seated Indians, watching them now with feelings that were close to affection. They are only children after all, he decided. Later on he was to wonder.

Fork-in-the-Tree made a sign and again the young brave moved forward, and placed a small bundle at Danny's feet. As the brave stooped to open the bundle, Pierre said quietly, "This is Wah-be-a-tik, White Elk. He is Sawaquot's son-in-law."

Danny watched the young man as he spread a small pile of furs on the ground. He must try to remember this man, but all of the Indians looked alike. White Elk was dressed much the same as the others. His scalp lock was thick with vermilion, and it was bound with the skin of a rattlesnake. Instead of hawk feathers, he wore a wing from a blue jay, and the brilliant blue feathers fluttered in the breeze as he bent to place the present at Danny's feet. Then he straightened, and with a tinkle of hawk bells, strode back to his place in the circle.

Danny quickly ran his hand through the thick pelts, making a quick guess of their worth. There were two others, fine ones, four marten, and about three pounds of beaver. All prime furs, worth about thirty shillings silver. Danny rose to his feet.

"We thank you, my brothers, for the rich furs you have

Seeing the gifts, the braves moved forward

brought. I wish now that you will take a present to seal our friendship and to show what we have brought for our friends, the Chippewa."

While Pierre translated, Danny lifted the stroud blankets, with their gifts of paint and gold braid. At the last minute Danny had added two silver bracelets to the bundle.

Seeing the gifts, the braves moved forward. Again came the cry of "Howh," and as Fork-in-the-Tree and White Elk reached the blankets, Danny handed one of the bracelets to the chief. Sawaquot accepted it in delight, and Danny handed the other to Wah-be-a-tik. The Indian took it and slipped it quickly over one muscular arm. Danny was glad he had brought the two. The expressions on their faces were worth the extra expense, even though the present of skins would nowhere near cover the cost.

Then, to Danny's surprise and relief, the Chippewa rose to their feet. The council was over. Danny stood watching them as they moved toward their canoes in a stately procession. A hand touched his shoulder. He turned and looked down into the smiling face of Pierre.

"You have done well, M'sieu. Jacques will be proud."

Before Danny could think of an answer, the old man gathered his coat about him and shuffled off.

Winter

AUGUST TURNED into September. Danny, busy in the post, helping Pierre make up the lists of credit given to the Indians, had little time to enjoy the beautiful north country around him. It was the first of November before he could take a musket and go out into the woods around the fort.

Winter was coming. For days now the wind had been growing sharper across the lake. The brilliant scarlet and yellow of autumn leaves lay deep along the path. To Danny, they looked like stained quills on a squaw's moccasins. After the visit of the Chippewa, all had gone smoothly. There were only a few traders at the fort and the last voyageur canoe had long since left for Superior or the lakes to the south. A few canoes had come up from Detroit, and Danny had hoped for a letter from home. None had come. At first he had felt badly, but now the new life was becoming so exciting that he thought little of the farm except during the lengthening evenings. His only touch with farming had been the small garden he had started outside the post. Pierre had suggested it. Winter meant food would be scarce and some potatoes would be welcome, the old man had said.

That night as Danny sat at his table with the account book, he began checking off the months before Jacques would return. Six months at the least, maybe seven if the ice remained longer in the lakes. But the time would pass fast enough, Danny thought. It hardly seemed possible that he had been at Michilimackinac since August. Danny moved the candle closer and opened his account book.

There were over twenty pages of credit entries, the last one dated October 15, 1762. The credit was to Pakko-sigon, which meant Indian tobacco. There were others elsewhere where Danny had written the translation of the Indian name or had merely put "first brother," or "father of three," or "Indian without nose." Under each name were listed the articles given. Powder and ball, blankets, tobacco, knife, traps, plain shirts, leggings, even handkerchiefs.

There were other items too: mirrors, hawk bells, vermilion. Danny wondered if this was cheating the Indians. Still, it was the practice of all traders. How else could the Indians be hired to bring in the furs of beaver, otter, mink, deer, bear, raccoon? Danny closed the book. It would soon be December and Christmas. Unless he went to the party given to the Indians at the commandant's, he would have to spend Christmas alone. Pierre would be in his house with his family, and he had said nothing about inviting Danny to come. Perhaps with Pierre's wife a Chippewa, they didn't celebrate Christmas. Danny thought of his mother and father in Detroit. He wondered if the O'Hara had slaughtered the hog. Perhaps for Christmas. Danny sighed and snuffed out the candle. Better to keep his mind on the store. Time enough to get excited about going home when the ice left the lakes.

Christmas came. Danny had spent the day sorting trade goods, staying close to the fire. Outside the snow still fell, hitting the one glazed-skin window at the front with a soft hissing sound. He put the last of the stroud blankets on its shelf and went to the window. The snow looked like a huge pale-blue trading blanket in the moonlight, lying flat on the ground, tucking the houses in snugly. Smaller ones draped the roofs.

Danny opened the door. A whirl of snow met him and Danny shivered. From the far end of the stockade, lights glowed yellow in the windows of the commandant's house. There was dancing there, and music from a fiddle. Danny hesitated. Jacques had told him about the parties at trading posts, where the rum turned the Indians into brawling, dangerous animals. Still, the soldiers would be there, and at least it would be better than sitting alone on Christmas night.

Danny closed the door and went into the back room. He lighted an extra candle and opened the lid of the horsehide trunk. His second pair of leggings hadn't been worn since the visit of the Chippewa. Danny undressed in growing excitement. Using water from melted snow, he bathed quickly and slipped into his fresh clothes. They felt strangely tight. He looked down over his leggings. They barely reached his ankles. It didn't seem possible. Danny pulled on his new shirt. The sleeves came high above his wrists. Strange, he hadn't noticed how he was growing. Danny undressed again quickly, and folding the clothes, took them into the front of the store to exchange them. By the time he found a pair of leggings, a shirt, moccasins, and capote that fitted, he was shivering with cold. He dressed quickly, then combed the snarl from his shoulder-length hair. His hair was again red. The last patch of black had been washed away weeks before.

At last he was ready. Danny looked down at his new deerskin leggings. His thighs, bare where the voyageur's leggings tied at the sides, were brown and hard, darker than the deerskin. Even the breechcloth was new. He had traded a string of blue beads to an Ottawa squaw for it. His sash, also new, was brilliant blue with red and yellow stripes running through it. Danny pulled the hood of his blue capote over his red wool cap, snuffed out the candles and unbolted the door. Closing it behind him, he locked it, dropping the key in his beaded sac-à-feu which hung from his belt, and headed for the house of the commandant.

He whistled an old carol as he walked along, moccasined feet sending little puffs of snow whirling up to meet the falling flakes. His new clothes were warm against his skin. No more patches for him, he thought. Jacques had said to help himself to any clothes in stock, but this was only the second time he had done so. With all of his clothing and food free, the pile of pelts that would be his in the spring would be all clear profit. How surprised his parents would be to see the wealth he had earned.

As the barracks and Indian house drew closer, Danny wondered about Jacques' warning. Rum had always been the main trading medium for furs. The French had tried to control it, but the Indians demanded the "white man's milk" as they called it, and the English, anxious to hold their newly won empire, were becoming more and more generous in their dispensing of it.

Danny remembered his father speaking of rum. What was it he had said? That feeding the Indians rum would soon have the "red divils" sinking the hatchet into every mother's son, or something like that. And yet, Captain Etherington had told him there would be no Indian trouble, and even Lieutenant Leslie had agreed. Danny wondered what his father had thought about the wampum belt he had mentioned in his note, the belt the Chippewa had been carrying on the day he ran away. Whatever the O'Hara decided, there had been no trouble. Probably the wampum belt hadn't been a war belt after all. Even the stories that had gone about the fort, telling of Indian unrest and poverty, had stopped. Captain Etherington had threatened to send the next bearer of wild tales to Albany in chains. Nevertheless, Danny felt his uneasiness grow as he heard the shouts coming from the commandant's house.

He walked cautiously up to the heavy door. His fingers were on the latch. Before he could lift the heavy iron, the door was flung violently open and Danny sprawled backward into the snow. A burst of sound rocked out of the brightly lighted interior. At the same time a half-naked Indian, his deerskins almost torn from his back, came charging out of the door. Behind him came a Huron buck, his painted face terrifying in the light of the open door. He leaped onto the back of the first Indian, his arm encircling the brave's throat. A tomahawk flashed red. They sprawled in the snow.

Danny rolled aside just in time; then he was on his

feet, running. He passed the door and caught a glimpse of the brawling figures inside. Someone shouted at him. Danny bent low and raced across the compound.

He reached the store panting, the shouts dim now at his back. He found his key and turned the lock. The door swung open. Danny leaped in and dropped the heavy bar. Grabbing his musket, he stood listening. There was no sound now except for the snow against the window. Cautiously, he lifted the bolt on the door and opening it a crack, peered through.

Lights still gleamed at the commandant's house. The front door had been closed, but something dark lay in the snow outside.

When Danny climbed into his bunk, he made sure his musket was close to his hand. He awoke once during the night, covered with perspiration. He had been dreaming that he was home in his mother's kitchen. His mother had just come in with a huge snow goose and had started plucking it. The white feathers were floating down like snow, covering everything. Suddenly the door had burst open and Captain Etherington had swept into the kitchen. "Daniel O'Hara," he had shouted. Then all at once it wasn't the captain at all, but Jacques. His clothes, hands, and face were dyed red. "Tête-Rouge," he shouted. "Your father has been killed by Pontiac." Danny had started up to touch the red clothes that Jacques wore. It wasn't dye that stained them, it was blood.

Danny sat up and tried to force the awful scene from his mind. Finally he threw back the blankets. Taking his musket, he went to the front door to test the bolt. When he finally crept back into the covers, sleep refused to come. He lay until morning, listening to the wind and the distant howling of wolves.

At last the sun was up. Danny, haggard from the night, stepped to the door for a kettle of snow for tea. This was the day he was to go fishing with Pierre. Danny looked toward the commandant's house. All was quiet. Even the mound that had lain at the front door was gone. Danny went back into the cabin and closed the door. Now, with the sun on the snow, the events of the night all seemed like a dream. Danny put snow on to boil while he dressed, chewing a handful of corn and thinking of the day ahead. He would have to hurry or Pierre would go without him, and he wanted some whitefish to eat. The deer was nearly gone and lake trout grew tiresome, but whitefish tasted good no matter how often he ate it. Pierre had shown him how to cook it. Pierre had learned the secret from his wife, Ahwun, Lady of the Mist. Thinking of Ahwun reminded Danny of little Annette, Pierre's and Ahwun's daughter. Danny had seen her only a few times.

He poured some boiling water from the pot over a few tea leaves in the bottom of his tin teapot. While it steeped he wondered if Annette would be with her father. Sometimes, he knew, they fished together. Hurrying now, Danny poured himself a cup of scalding tea and munched another handful of parched corn. Annette was small and slender, like her father, without the heaviness of so many Indian women. Her skin was fair and her eyes, while they slanted a little over her high cheekbones, were as blue as Danny's. Annette, Danny decided, was beautiful.

He drained his cup, pulled on his capote, mittens, and cap, and went out the front door, locking it behind him.

The sun was blinding on the snow. Danny squinted his eyes in the glare and headed for Pierre's cabin. The old man was waiting for him when Danny reached the shore. He was alone. Well, Danny thought, a girl shouldn't go fishing anyway.

"Hallo!" Danny waved his mittened hand. Pierre waved back. As Danny ran up he saw that the old habitant had a net, a pole, and a long line. Danny looked at the strange fishing gear in amazement. How could they catch fish with a net when the lake was frozen almost to the horizon?

"Bonjour, mon ami." Smiling broadly, Pierre touched his fur cap. "I thought you had forgotten."

"I overslept," Danny said.

"So. You were perhaps at the dance last night?" Pierre winked.

"Well," Danny said, "I did go over, but I didn't stay long."

"Bien. It is best." Pierre's old eyes were suddenly serious. "Did you sleep early and well?"

"Not too well, Pierre." Danny didn't know what to say.

The grizzled Canadian seemed to be asking for information, but Danny wondered if he should tell of the fight he had witnessed. Sometimes in the North, Jacques had said, it was better not to see things.

Pierre seemed satisfied. "It is of no matter," he said. "You did not see it then. But four were stabbed last night. Two Ottawa, one Huron, and a squaw. Also, a child fell into a fire and was burned. But it is always so when there is rum. Let us fish."

"With that?" Danny pointed to the net, anxious to forget the night.

"And why not, M'sieu?" Pierre smiled.

"But the lake is frozen."

"You shall see, Danny." Pierre handed Danny the pole with its coil of rope. They started across the ice, working their way carefully over the huge mounds, brown with blown sand, that lined the shore, then on to where the ice was smooth.

Pierre stopped. Laying his net on the ice, he began to

chop a hole with his ax. Danny watched, puzzled, as Pierre took the pole and, using it as a measuring stick, chopped four more holes a pole's length apart. Stationing Danny at the second hole, the old man tied a line to the end of the willow pole and, thrusting his hand into the black, icy water of the first hole, pushed the stick with the line up under the ice to where Danny was standing. Danny stooped and seized the pole, still puzzled as to how they could use the net. Again the pole was thrust under the ice to the third hole until the line was completely hidden in the water, except for the far end which Pierre had weighted securely, and the line that he held.

Pierre then tied the net tightly to the line. Handing it to Danny, he walked back to the first hole and began to pull on the rope. As the net slid through Danny's hand, he began to understand.

The rest was easy. As soon as the net was under the ice, the large stones on the sinking line at each end pulled the mesh down toward bottom, while the floats along the top spread the net neatly into a trap.

The sun was setting when they finally pulled the net in. Icy water ran down Danny's arms, but he was too busy watching the gleaming whitefish that flopped helplessly in the mesh to care. It took them almost until dark to drag the rapidly freezing fish across the ice to shore. Chilled but happy, Danny took his share of the fish back to the cabin and hung them from poles outside the door to freeze solid. When he finally went in to sit before the fire and dry his clothes, he knew with a sense of relief that he had enough food to last until spring.

Jacques Again

THE NEW YEAR came: 1763. In the following weeks, Danny spent his time in hunting, repairing gear, and learning the Algonquin tongue from Old Pierre. At night he wrote in his journal the events of the day so that Jacques, on his return, would know all that had happened in his absence. He even made candles, using the grease from the game he had killed. Not having a candle mold, he dipped them instead.

He was often lonely. A few Indians dropped in with furs, but as the spring drew closer, Danny realized that more and more were coming into the fort. His pile of furs was growing. He had several large bundles wrapped carefully in the storeroom. Every morning now, upon rising, he would go to the door and look toward the lake, hoping for the first sign of the spring breakup.

It came on the second of April, a little early. Danny heard the booming of the ice one morning and knew that Jacques should be back in a few weeks. From then until the twelfth, Danny spent all the time he could spare on the guard walk of the stockade, watching the horizon.

He sighted the canoes late on the afternoon of the twelfth of April. They looked like drifting black ducks against the sun. With a shout, Danny scampered down the ladder and raced for the beach. The canoes came closer. Danny, standing first on one foot and then the other, was hardly able to keep from firing his musket into the air. He could see the lead canoe clearly, Henri in the bow.

It wasn't until they were within gunshot of the beach that Danny realized that Jacques wasn't with them. He waited in an agony of suspense and finally called Jacques' name. It was the young pork eater who answered. Jacques had gone on to Detroit. He had taken his small canoe after more trade goods. Danny turned away. All the loneliness that he had kept down during the winter welled up in him now. The walls of the fort blurred in front of his eyes.

Trade began in earnest the next morning. Hardly a day passed without Indians standing about the place, cautiously choosing trinkets or bringing in loads of furs and renewing their credit. The pages of Danny's account book were filling fast. He scarcely had time at night to write in his journal after a day of haggling over pelts. Several times canoes were sighted, bringing the whole fort down to the waterfront. But Jacques wasn't among them. Even the men began to grumble. They were eager to go on to Montreal and home. Finally, Danny decided he could wait no longer. Suppose something had happened to Jacques? He made up his mind to go to Detroit himself. He could take Henri and a small crew with one of the north canoes. It would mean paying them extra wages, but Danny felt as though he could wait no longer.

The following day he took his musket, loaded it with swan shot in case the geese were flying, and headed for

Pierre's. He would ask the old man to watch the post while he was gone.

Reaching the beach, Danny stood there for a moment watching the waves pounding the shore. They looked like charging dragoons, white plumes waving as they broke ranks on the sand, then re-formed to attack again. A whistle of wings made him look up. He half raised his gun. But the geese were out of range—the old honker at the head of the flock had seen Danny and was leading the others across the lake.

Suddenly Danny saw a black speck bobbing far out on the water. Grounding his musket, he shaded his eyes with his hand, hardly daring to hope. The speck grew into a canoe with a single figure at the paddle. The canoe moved closer and Danny jerked his musket to his shoulder and fired into the air—Jacques had come at last!

"Halloo, Danny!"

"Jacques!" Danny shouted back, waving his arms and doing a crazy war dance on the sand. He rammed another charge into the barrel of his musket and fired again; then, raising the still smoking gun over his head, he plunged into the surf and waded out till he could grasp the bow of the canoe. Laying his gun across the thwarts, Danny seized the gunwale and shoved. Jacques dipped his paddle hard, and the canoe rolled with the breakers straight up onto the beach. Black beard flying, teeth flashing, Jacques leaped to the sand and threw his arms about Danny in a bear hug.

"Ah, Danny, Jacques is glad to see you." He stepped back and seized Danny by the shoulders. "You have grown tall and your hair is red. Tête-Rouge again, eh?"

Raising the still smoking gun, he plunged into the surf

"I thought you were never coming, Jacques. Did you see my folks? What is happening at Detroit?"

"Your papa and maman are well—they send you their best wishes. Now, help me with my gear and we will talk."

Grinning happily, Danny took Jacques' gun and his own; then, tugging at the thongs of one huge pack, he started after Jacques.

"What is in this pack, Jacques? It weighs a ton."

"Trade good, trade good, Red Head. I thought that yours would be about gone and I bought all I could."

Danny hoisted the pack to his shoulder. A surge of questions was bubbling up inside of him, but he wanted to wait until he and Jacques were alone inside the store. Jacques, however, was filled with questions too, and as with a true bourgeois, they were about business.

"How many pelts, Commis?" Jacques asked.

Danny answered proudly, glad to show how much he had learned. "I'm not too sure of the exact figure, Jacques, but we have around a hundred fifty packs of beaver—that's fifteen thousand pounds—twenty packs of marten and thirty otter."

Jacques whistled. "Magnifique! Never have I done better. What are they worth, eh, Commis?"

"About seven thousand dollars in beaver and about one thousand in marten and otter. Maybe more, Jacques."

"Oho! It was a lucky day when you ran away, Danny, lucky for your bourgeois, and from your looks, lucky for you. My little redhead is almost as big as Jacques! But enough. What are trade goods bringing?"

Danny started to answer, but they were inside the fort

now and other traders kept calling out greetings to the huge Canadian. It wasn't until they were in the small room at the back that Danny proudly pulled his ledger from the shelf. "See, Jacques, I have kept the books just as you asked. Here are all the prices."

"Read it to me, Danny." Jacques sank down on Danny's bunk. The rope springs creaked and sagged as Jacques leaned his huge bulk back and filled his pipe.

Danny held his book close to the window and began. "One gun, twenty beaver. Stroud blanket, ten; white blanket, eight; ax, three; half pint gunpowder, one; ten balls, one. Tobacco, that is, Spenser's twist, one skin a foot, rum, two skins, depending on the amount of water in it."

"Aha! You are a real commis. And to prove it, I am ready to give you your share, Danny."

"My share?" Danny let the ledger slide onto the table. In the excitement of Jacques' coming, he had forgotten all about his wages.

"Of course, Daniel. That is what you worked for, no?"

"Well," Danny looked down at his moccasin, "I guess so, Jacques. All through the winter I kept thinking about it, but when spring came and you didn't come with the others. . . ." Danny hesitated.

"Go on, Danny. You were angry?"

"No, it wasn't that, Jacques, honest." Danny looked at his friend. "I guess," he stammered, "I finally realized I came so I could be like you, Jacques."

"Oho! That is it, eh, Commis? Trying to soften up your bourgeois so he will give you more."

"No, honest. . . ." Danny flushed.

Jacques threw back his great head and roared with laughter. "Do not take Jacques serious, mon ami. I have long since decided what you shall have. Ten packs of beaver!"

"Ten packs!" Danny's mouth dropped open. "Why, that is a thousand dollars!" He stared at Jacques, wondering if it was really true. That was as much as an experienced bowsman made!

"Is that not enough? Why don't you say something, Red Head?"

"Enough? Faith, Jacques, it's more than enough." Danny's eyes were shining.

"Good, it is done. It was my lucky day when you decided not to become a farmer."

Danny scuffed the toe of his moccasin along the plank floor. That was the sweetest praise he had ever heard.

"Now, Danny," he said, "I will tell you of my journey.

"After trading south along Lake Michigan, I left my brigade in March and crossed overland on snowshoes to Fort Detroit. My cabin was still snug, but one of my two canoes had a hole in the bow. So I left it there and took the other one down-river to see your maman and papa."

"Were they awfully angry?" Danny asked.

Jacques' eyes twinkled. "Angry! Have you ever seen a lynx in action? Your papa was that quick! I had no more walked into the farm till he was at my throat, so! Even before I could speak, he leaped upon me. Name of a name!" Jacques' chair came down to the floor with a bang. He slapped his thigh and roared, remembering the look on the O'Hara's pink face.

"How a little man can be so strong, Danny, is more

than I understand. His fingers were like iron on my throat, and I could not catch my breath. Then, just as I made up my mind that I must catch him, so, and crush him, your maman came in the door!

"It is very funny now, but not so funny then, I can tell you. Your maman, she came in the door like a she-bear and grabbed O'Hara and pulled hard. Then she started talking to us. *Oho!* How she did lash us with her tongue. Then it was over—just like that—and we were sitting in your kitchen drinking a glass of your papa's cider. And Danny, after I told him that you were my partner and left him a pack of four beaver, he was all at once a very happy man and insisted that I stay for supper."

"Did you tell them when we would be back?" asked Danny.

"I said we would leave here the first of June and spend the summer at Fort Detroit, if that is all right with you?"

"That's wonderful, Jacques!" Danny's face glowed with happiness. Going home again, and with ten packs of beaver! Suddenly he remembered his letter. "What did my father say about the Chippewa I wrote him of?"

Jacques grinned. "He said the 'divils' were up to no good and that he had told Major Rogers and Major Gladwyn, the commandant. Gladwyn had refused to listen, your father said, but Rogers had a great deal of respect for Pontiac; and if it is true that the Chippewa were carrying black and purple wampum, it could mean war. I have heard that Pontiac is trying to unite the tribes through all the Northwest. He cannot be blamed, Danny, for this. He has seen his lands taken by the English. Under the French he was happy, but not so with the English. It may be his plan to drive all the English from the country so that once more the lands of his people will be free. And so the wampum could have been a message belt from Pontiac. But," Jacques yawned, "I do not think you should worry. The Indian is our red brother, and now he comes in huge numbers around the fort to trade. But it is always this way."

"Captain Etherington says that they will stay peaceful and he must be right, Jacques. Anyway, Detroit has a strong garrison, hasn't it?"

"Strong enough, Danny. Now, let us look at the goods I have brought. Tomorrow my canoes go up to Montreal without me. I shall see them in Detroit, come fall. We perhaps may not be able to stay all summer in Detroit, but two months at least. Next fall when you come back here, you won't mind being host to all the Chippewa, eh, Danny?"

Danny shook his head, remembering. "I was sort of scared, Jacques. . . ."

"So I heard. I would have loved to have seen you make that speech." Jacques threw back his head and roared.

Danny couldn't help but grin, then in a moment they were both holding their sides shouting with laughter.

Neither knew that this was the last time they would ever laugh together.

Treachery and Disaster

THE FIRST of June, 1763, came and went. Trade had been so brisk that they decided to wait one day more. It seemed as though all of the Indians in the Northwest Territory were anxious to buy hatchets and powder and ball. Many had moved up north from their winter's hunting, and their supplies, they said, were running low. The Indians stood about the store, peering at the silver bracelets and the beads and blankets, talking among themselves and asking for credit against next year's beaver. Danny was growing impatient. The red men were drifting in and out in increasing numbers, but they were not buying. Almost all of them said they would be back the next day.

It was not until the third of June, two days before the king's birthday, that Danny started to pack the furs and put the trade goods away in the heavy cupboards. He had just finished wrapping his new clothes to carry them down to the canoe when a shadow fell across the floor. Danny didn't look up at first. He thought it was Jacques returning from the lake where he had gone to watch an incoming canoe that had been sighted.

The shadow grew larger and Danny glanced up. It was a very short, very dirty Indian who stood there gazing at Danny with dull black eyes.

"Boozhoo, Englishman." He spoke in Chippewa.

"Boozhoo. Greetings." Danny answered in the same tongue.

"I have come, Englishman, to ask you to attend a great game of Baggitiway that the Chippewa are going to play against the Sac nation for high wager. The English captain will bet on the Chippewa. How will you bet?"

Danny stood up and muttered something about leaving for Detroit.

"You must come, Englishman. It will be a great contest." The Indian turned and strode out the door.

Danny watched him go. The Indian wore the fringed shirt of a Wyandotte. He wondered what a Wyandotte was doing so far from Detroit. Something else puzzled Danny—the voice had sounded familiar, but the Indian's face had been daubed so heavily with paint that his features were lost in the clay and grease. Danny shook his head and bent down to finish packing. He would ask Jacques when he returned.

Baggitiway, thought Danny, would be fun to watch. Jacques had told him about it, describing the game, only he called it "la crosse." The Indians played it often, betting huge sums on the outcome. They used a bat about four feet long, curved and ending in a sort of racquet. Two posts were planted in the ground almost a mile apart, and the two teams started the ball in the middle, then tried to send it toward their own goal. Danny wished he had time to watch.

The morning passed slowly; the tribes were gathering outside the fort and still Jacques hadn't returned. Danny had just taken down his musket and was preparing to go out to find him when a wild chorus of shouts sounded from outside the fort. Danny stepped to the door and looked toward the gate. He saw a ball sailing over the walls, and in a moment a great crowd of naked Indians streaked in the gates, chasing it. Danny watched idly, wishing that he could join the game.

Suddenly the huge figure of Jacques burst through the crowd and came pounding up to the cabin. In another instant he had pushed Danny inside and slammed the door. His face was gray above his dark beard, and Danny watched him in amazement as he stood gasping for breath.

"The canoe!" Jacques gasped out the words and pointed toward the lake. "It has brought bad news—Pontiac has attacked Detroit!"

"It can't be true!" Danny found his voice. "Not just when we are ready to go home!" He thought of the wampum belt he had seen. Why hadn't someone listened? They had been carrying the war belt, and nobody listened!

There was a wild yelling outside. Danny clutched Jacques' arm. It was the war whoop!

Together they unbarred the door and flung it open.

A great mob of howling savages were swarming into the fort, cutting down every Englishman they saw! Danny cried out and pulled back the hammer on his flintlock. Jacques swung his arm wide and knocked the gun to the floor.

"Don't be a fool. You can do nothing against a thousand savages except bring them here!"

Clutching the doorway, unable to move, Danny stared in sick horror. He kept waiting for the drumbeat to arms. It never came. Redcoats were spilling out of the block-house only to be struck down like toy soldiers. Lieutenant Jemette shouted an order. Instantly he was seized by a yelling savage and knocked down. A hatchet flashed. The horror went on—Englishman after Englishman fell to the ground under the merciless hatchets to lie motion-less, their scalped heads white against spreading pools of red.

Danny saw Jacques' face close to his own. "Get back! You must hide!" His voice was hoarse.

Danny felt himself being thrust back behind the counter. He huddled down in a kind of dream, closing his eyes to shut out the horror of Lieutenant Jemette's murder.

The yells were louder! Jacques' huge frame filled the doorway as he watched the running savages. There was the sudden rasp of moccasins on the floor, then Jacques' calm voice raised in answer to the excited voices of In-dians. "There is no Englishman here, no Englishman here, I tell you." He kept repeating it over and over. The voices grew fainter and Danny began to hope.

Then he heard a new voice. It was the voice of the Wyandotte who had asked him to the game, but the voice had changed and it was speaking in *French!*

"So, Le Blanc, there is no Englishman here. Now we shall see who hits Joe Loup and lives to tell about it."

A great crash rocked the counter. Jacques' voice rose in a bellow. "Run, Danny, run. . . ."

Danny pulled his hatchet from his belt. His musket lay

Jacques was struggling with a surging mass of red men

useless on the floor. Jacques was roaring in rage. There was no place to run, and Jacques needed help.

As Danny's head cleared the counter, he looked straight into the huge bulk of a looting Indian. Danny raised his hatchet and brought it crashing down on the painted head with all his might. A great jet of red spurted over him. He pulled the hatchet free, feeling the weight of the Indian against his legs. Danny stepped over the body and raised his ax again.

Jacques was struggling with a surging mass of red men. His huge hands grasped Danny's musket by the barrel, and as he swung it in shattering circles, heads were splitting like ripe melons. All at once, Danny saw the stunted figure of Joe Loup. He was moving stealthily toward Jacques, trying to get at his back. With a shout of warning to Jacques, Danny threw his hatchet. It whizzed straight for the snarling face. Joe ducked! The flashing blade chunked harmlessly into the wall. In the next instant, Joe Loup dived beneath the terrible musket, and Danny cried out in terror. He saw the flash of a knife. Joe's arm rose and fell. Again his arm rose. This time the knife was crimson and he held it in both hands. Down went the knife into Jacques' back. Jacques staggered, caught himself, slid to the floor, and lay still.

Before Danny could move, he felt his arms twisted violently from behind. There was a blinding flash, a deafening report, and Joe Loup stepped back from the limp body of what had once been Danny's friend.

Danny screamed Jacques' name twice! Joe raised the butt of his pistol and stepped through the gun smoke toward Danny. Then blackness came.

Captured

DANNY OPENED his eyes. There was a blinding pain in his head, and his legs felt raw where he had been dragged across the compound. He tried to sit up. Waves of dizziness sent him reeling back, flat on the hard earth floor.

From where he lay he could see other figures seated motionless in the half-dark of a room. He was able to make out the shocked white faces of Ezekiel Solomon, the trader, and some soldiers. No one spoke, and from outside the door came the drunken shouts of looting savages. His father's voice came back to him then: "Have you seen what rum does to Indians?"

Danny closed his eyes. Jacques was dead; Detroit was under siege. This must be the end—the end of his world.

"So, Englishman!"

Danny raised his head. Joe Loup stood in the open doorway.

"You are not dead. You can thank Joe Loup for saving your life—my red brothers would have lifted your hair."

Danny couldn't answer.

Joe grasped Danny's long hair and pulled him to his feet. Danny stumbled blindly against the wall, fighting for balance. Joe pushed him out the door. It was nearly dark. Danny fell to his knees, and again the man jerked him to his feet. A knife dug into his back.

"Come along, Englishman. You are my prisoner."

The knife forced him along into the shadows.

"Now, off with your coat, Englishman!" Joe spat. "The night grows cold and Joe Loup needs new clothes."

Danny tugged blindly at his sash and let the coat fall from his shoulders. Joe snatched it up. A chill wind wailed through the fort. Danny shivered. Slowly he felt his strength returning.

Joe's twisted lips were grinning like a goblin's as he pulled the new coat over his red-streaked shirt, covering the stains of dried blood. Again the knife found Danny's back, piercing the thin shirt, driving the strength from his legs so that he nearly fell.

They were moving away from the center of the stockade. Pointed log walls threw back shadows from the setting sun like rows of jagged teeth. The knife kept him on his feet, but slowly the insistent pricking began to drive the despair from his mind. In its place came anger.

"Where are you taking me?" Danny's voice was hoarse.

"Ah, the Englishman is afraid. I am taking you outside the fort"—the knife dug deeper—"to kill you."

Danny stumbled over something. He realized with horror that it was a corpse. Hopelessness came back to him, drowning his anger in a flood of fear. To die here, he thought, never to see his parents again, and all because of men who refused to face the truth. And so, men had died. Men like Jacques, and maybe his father; women like his mother, who wanted peace. And he knew that his father had been right—peace was not something you thought about or just took for the asking. Sometimes you had to fight for peace!

His shoulders slumped. Joe dug the knife deeper. It was then that Danny knew that he couldn't die—not yet. There was too much that he had to finish—and first he must finish Joe Loup.

Danny steeled himself against the piercing knife and stopped. "Why don't you kill me now, Joe?"

Joe laughed. "Ha! So, you *are* afraid. I will wait a bit, Englishman." The knife eased a little. This time Danny only pretended to stumble. Joe seized him by the collar. Now! Danny fell forward, pulling Joe off balance. In a flash, Danny spun around, twisting Joe's left hand in the strong collar of his shirt. The man lurched forward; Danny seized the wrist that held the knife and twisted it back up under Joe's shoulder blades. Joe grunted with

pain and dropped the knife. With all his strength, Danny shoved the wrist upward. Something snapped, and Joe Loup fell to his knees, screaming. Danny reached for the knife.

There was a sudden yell at his back. Three Indians were coming straight for him, yelling and waving their tomahawks. Danny whirled and raced for the gates, expecting every moment to feel an ax between his shoulders.

He pounded out of the fort and into the darkness. Pierre's cabin lay dead ahead. Danny plunged into the shallows of the lake and fell flat on his stomach. He lay there, gathering strength, then, as no sound of pursuit came from the fort, he crawled ashore, ran in a half crouch to the cabin and pounded on the door. There was a dim light showing through the cracks, and Danny prayed that Pierre would answer.

"Who is there?"

Danny went weak with relief—it was Pierre's voice.

"It's Danny O'Hara, Pierre. Help me, for the love of God!"

He could hear the heavy bar being lifted, then the door swung open. Danny stepped quickly in and closed the door behind him. The room was lighted by a single lamp, and Old Pierre was gazing at him in a sort of disbelief.

Danny started to speak, then he saw a tall figure in the shadows at Pierre's back. Danny's knees buckled and he slid to the floor, unconscious. The figure moved into the lamplight—it was Fork-in-the-Tree, chief of the Chippewa!

Annette

W HEN DANNY opened his eyes, sunlight was flooding the room. At first he thought that he was safe in Pierre's house. Suddenly, he remembered Fork-in-the-Tree. Danny sat up, and as the blanket fell from his bare shoulders, he felt flashes of pain across his back. He bit his lips and stared down at the strips of cloth that bound him.

Then a cool hand was on his shoulder, pressing him gently back on the bed. Annette stood over him, her eyes red from crying.

"Where is Sawaquot?" Danny whispered.

"Shh; you must be quiet and rest." Annette laid her fingers across his lips. "Sawaquot is my uncle and our friend. Papa sent for him to find you when we learned of the massacre." She tried to smile. "We wanted to warn you, but they would not let us, and we hoped that Jacques could save you."

"Jacques is dead."

"We know." Annette's eyes filled with fresh tears. "Papa has gone there now to bury him. He will bring fresh clothes for you."

Danny looked at the girl, hoping to shut out the horrors that he had seen. She lowered her eyes under his steady gaze, but Danny found peace in watching her. Annette's black hair hung in soft waves about her fair-skinned face. It was braided Indian-fashion, but it had none of the coarse stringiness of Indian hair. Her long lashes lifted, and Danny found himself gazing deep into her blue eyes. He was surprised to see a flush spreading over her cheeks.

"What is it, Annette? You have been crying. Is it because of Jacques?"

She nodded. "And something else."

"Tell me what it is."

Before Danny could say any more, she burst into sobs and fled from the room.

"Annette!" Danny tried to rise. The door was pushed open and Pierre came in to stand beside his bed.

"You called, Daniel?"

"Did you find Jacques?" Danny avoided Pierre's sad eyes and lay back on the bed.

"Yes. The good Jesuit father from L'Arbre Croche helped me bury him. He was not scalped, Danny." The old man's eyes filled with tears.

Danny couldn't answer.

"But now." Pierre wiped his eyes without shame. "We must think of you. Do you feel strong enough to stand?"

"I must stand, Pierre. Somehow, I must get to Detroit. They need me!"

"You cannot go, Danny. The Chippewa will not permit it. I tried to buy your freedom, but Sawaquot does not dare to let you go."

"But can't you help me to escape?" Danny forced himself to sit up.

The old man shook his head sadly. "You must go with the Chippewa."

Danny stared at Pierre in horror. Now he knew why Annette had been crying. He was a captive!

Pierre spoke kindly. "It will not be too bad, my son. At least you are alive, and that is a miracle. If you had not escaped from Joe Loup, you would be dead; and if you had stayed in the prison. . . ." The old man shrugged and shook his head.

After a while Danny looked up to see Annette and her mother standing at his side. Ahwun looked at Danny and smiled.

"You are fortunate that you have good friend, M'sieu. My small Annette, she is very sorry to see you go, but she knows that we see you again. You will be safe with my brother, the great Sawaquot. He has promised it, and someday you will return to us. Is that not so, Annette?"

Annette looked down at her beaded moccasins and was silent.

"Listen, Danny." Pierre made what he hoped was a comic face. "Annette cried all night and would let no one else take care of you. We were not even allowed near, were we, Maman?"

"I did not cry very much, Papa, only when. . . ." She broke off and stood biting her lip.

"Only when you learned that Danny would be gone for a while." Pierre winked at Danny.

"Oh, Papa!" Annette's face was flaming.

Danny began to feel a little better. Things could not be so bad—not when Pierre could joke about it. He looked at Annette and managed to smile.

Slowly the girl's face changed, and she smiled back shyly.

"Now!" Pierre was delighted. "Now you women must leave." He shooed them with his hands. "Do not come back until I call. Danny and I have much to do before he can be a Chippewa!"

"A Chippewa? What do you mean, Pierre?"

"Why, Danny, you are to become an Indian."

Danny groaned. "Not all that stain again?"

"Do not groan. It will save your life." Pierre took a razor from its case and gave Annette a gentle push toward the door. She stopped to glance back at Danny, and he waved at her. She smiled happily and followed her mother out of the room.

As soon as the door closed, Pierre reached over and grasped Danny's long hair. "Hold still now, Red Head. It is a shame, but it must come off." He began to slice through the red locks. Danny watched the great hunks of hair falling to the floor. He wondered if he would ever be just Danny O'Hara again. First a Canadian, now an Indian. He glanced at the pile of clothing that Pierre had brought. His musket and shot and powder horn were there too. At least he wouldn't be an unarmed captive. When his chance came to escape, he would be ready!

After it was all over, Danny stood up and begged for a mirror. While Pierre went to find one, Danny looked down at himself. He wore a long fringed shirt, painted in bold designs. A collar of wampum hung about his neck, another on his chest. Both arms had large bands of silver above the elbow and at the wrist, and his legs were covered with *mitasses*, leggings of scarlet. Over all of this he wore a brilliant red blanket. Danny raised his hand and ran his fingers over his scalp. It had been shaved, all

except for a spot on the crown where the long hair stood straight up, stiff with grease. Pierre had said the color was good—many tribesmen wore vermilion in their hair.

He was anxious to see his face. Pierre had spent almost an hour carefully mixing vermilion and charcoal and white clay to paint designs across his forehead and around his nose and even down his neck. Then he had taken three hawk feathers and had tied them tight to Danny's scalp lock.

Danny smiled, thinking how Pierre had stood back to

admire his work with one eye closed and his tongue sticking out from the corner of his mouth. "You are a perfect savage," he had said. "Your name shall be Misquah, the Red-haired One."

"Misquah." Danny said it aloud. He rather liked his new name. Misquah, the Chippewa. Pierre had told him that he was being adopted by Sawaquot because Fork-in-the-Tree had lost his brother during the war. Adopted after having all of his white blood washed away in the lake! Danny couldn't believe it, but Pierre had said it was so. While he had been unconscious the night before, Pierre and Sawaquot had taken him to the lake and had washed him.

Well, Danny thought, at least I'm still alive. It would certainly be better being Sawaquot's brother than his prisoner, and he wouldn't be prisoner for long!

Danny wrinkled up his face. His skin felt hard and heavy with the paint. He wished that Pierre would come with that mirror.

There was a sudden commotion in the doorway. Danny turned to see Annette and her mother staring at him. Annette began to giggle. Danny straightened, pretending anger, and stalked toward her, scowling.

"Who dares to laugh at Misquah, the great warrior?"

Annette shrieked and tried to run away. Danny seized her by the arms, laughing. She stared up at him, her eyes wide.

"Oh, Danny," she wailed, "you are too *real* an Indian!"

"Oho! What did you expect?" Pierre shouted with laughter. "Now, boy, look at yourself!"

Danny, suddenly embarrassed, dropped his hands

from Annette's arms and took the mirror. He turned toward the light and looked into the glass. He was shocked at what he saw. All trace of Danny O'Hara was gone. In his place was a savage brave. Broad streaks of vermilion slashed across his cheeks, while two lines of black on either side of his mouth gave his face a look of cunning cruelty. Even his blue eyes seemed black as they stared out through the circles of white clay. He wrinkled his forehead, showed his teeth, and scowled. The face in the mirror grimaced horribly, and Annette giggled again.

Then he felt Pierre's hand on his shoulder. "Come, Danny. Sawaquot is waiting."

Danny tucked the mirror into his paint pouch. Be brave, he told himself, and took Pierre's outstretched hand. The old man's eyes were wet as he turned away. Maman came next. Pulling his head down, she reached up and kissed him loudly on both cheeks. As she drew back, Danny saw that some of his paint had come off on her round face. Somehow it didn't seem funny to Danny.

Annette was last. She held out her small hand gravely, as she had seen her father do. Her soft palm was warm and it clung to his fingers. Then Danny O'Hara lifted shot pouch, powder horn, and musket from Pierre's hands, pulled his blanket about him, and strode out the door.

Sawaquot was waiting. Still no one said a word. But Danny knew that he had another home waiting for him. Somehow he would have to return.

Danny walked straight for the waiting chief, not daring to look back at his friends. He must be Danny O'Hara no longer, but Misquah, the Chippewa.

"Boozhoo!" Sawaquot greeted him calmly.

"Boozhoo!" Danny answered him.

"Come, my brother, you are welcome in my lodge." Fork-in-the-Tree moved toward the fort. Danny followed, amazed. Sawaquot had smiled when he greeted him. He is human after all, thought Danny; as human as Pierre.

They walked through the fort in silence. Fork-in-the-Tree's lodge was at the far end, and Danny was glad when they took the side path. He was able to avoid the store that had been Jacques'. As they walked, Danny felt his confidence mount. Indians were everywhere, but they gave him only a casual glance, then went back to their tasks.

Sawaquot stopped in front of a round-topped lodge covered with bark. Raising the skin flap that served for a door, he motioned for Danny to enter.

"Be seated, Misquah. I go to attend a great council." He lifted the skin door and was gone.

Almost at once the lodge was filled with noisy women. They came bringing bowls of maize mixed with bear fat, and Danny ate ravenously. It was the first food he had tasted in over thirty hours. He called for another bowl, and the Indian women giggled and laughed. They kept pointing to his bracelets and leggings. "Meno, meno," they said. Danny dug into the second bowl and smiled. They thought he was handsome.

As he scraped the sides of the dish clean, he tried to talk with the women. The eldest, he knew, must be Sawaquot's wife. Her name was Wah-bu-noong, Lady from the East. But try as he would, he could learn little else.

When Danny had finished his third bowl of food, he got to his feet. The women ignored him now. Danny lifted the flap of the bark wigwam and stepped out. The council was in session. All the men of the tribe were seated in a huge circle in the center of the encampment. Their backs were to him. Sawaquot stood in the center of the circle, speaking. His tall figure was erect, his eyes flashing, as he spoke slowly and with great dignity. Danny moved closer. He caught the word "Michilimackinac." At first Danny thought they must be speaking of the fort. Then he saw Fork-in-the-Tree's arm sweep northward. The hand pointed toward the island, blue on the distant horizon. Sawaquot paused. There were cries of "Meno. Good. We go, we go." Another brave jumped to his feet and began a speech. But Danny wasn't listening. He knew now that the tribe was going to the Island of the Great Turtle.

His heart sank. Once they had left the mainland, his chances for escape would be slim. Why not just walk away from the lodge while the council was busy with their powwow? Danny started around the side of the wigwam. He wanted to run, but he made himself go slowly. Suddenly he realized that his musket was inside the bark hut. He hesitated. To go on unarmed would be dangerous, and yet the council might break up at any moment. Quickly he turned back toward the wigwam. Lifting the flap, he slipped inside. The squaws were at the far end of the darkened hut. He snatched up his musket and slipped out the door.

"It is too late for hunting!" Sawaquot was coming toward him. The council was over. Danny let the musket slide through his hands. The butt touched the ground. He had missed his chance for escape.

Fork-in-the-Tree came up. Quietly, almost gently, he took the flintlock from Danny's unresisting fingers. In broken French he said, "Misquah, you must not try to escape again. Our young men guard every corner. If even our own people should try to leave, they would be stopped. Do not forget, we feel the tread of many moccasins on our trail. My people are now in great fear. If you wish to live, you must forget escape." The chief stooped and entered the lodge.

For a moment Danny stood looking longingly toward the gates of the fort, thronging now with painted, savage Chippewa. Then he followed Sawaquot into the lodge.

The bark wigwam was taken down at noon. Danny stood by and watched the old women packing the iron pots, the blankets, and the gear toward the beached canoes.

Indian dogs snarled and snapped at each other as they raced through the fort. Danny, at the chief's side, moved slowly at the end of a long line of warriors and passed through the gates without raising his head. Down across the grassy entrance to the fort moved the noisy procession, down onto the sand where birch canoes were thick along the water's edge. The canoes were filled to the gunwales with bark lodges, weapons, pots, blankets, children, women, and dogs. Danny found himself in a canoe with ten other young men and the chief. He had no time to think of escape now. Every thought must be of himself if he were to pass as a Chippewa brave. With a great shout, the three hundred fighting men of the tribe shoved the canoes into the breakers. They were off toward the island.

Danny dared not look back toward the fort until they were well out from shore. Only then did he glance over his shoulder. The log walls looked the same as always, without a hint of the terror that had struck. Only the English flag was missing from the pine pole. For a brief moment, Danny imagined that he was still in a voyageur's canoe. Then his eyes focused again on the ten copper backs ahead of him, heavy with bear grease and paint. His hand came up and touched his own shaven head. Fiercely he dug his paddle into the water. He was Misquah! He must be, or he wouldn't live to see another sun. The flotilla spread out ahead in the blazing noon like some nightmare army. Danny bit his lips and paddled on.

The blur on the horizon grew more humped, more turtlelike. A sudden wind sprang up out of the northeast. Racing dark clouds dimmed the sun. Slowly the lake changed from blue to green, then to an ugly gray.

The waves rose, white-crested, angry. Danny forgot everything but paddling. Following the beat of the bowsman, the paddlers no longer drove the canoe on with regular, timed strokes, but held their paddles when they met a charging wave. Only when they hit the crest did they drive the red blades deep, sending the light canoes skimming into the trough of the next roller. They bobbed on toward the island like a flock of loons. The frail craft rode each swell easily.

There was a sudden gust of wind. The canoe veered, then plunged its prow deep into a large comber. A great drenching wall of green crashed down into the canoe.

Danny caught his breath, but the light craft righted itself and plunged on. Instantly a squaw in the next canoe seized a dog tied snarling at her feet. With a cry she threw the helpless animal into the water. A loud wailing went up from the paddling Chippewa. Danny caught the word "Manitou," repeated over and over.

The paddlers redoubled their efforts, feeling sure that the offended spirit would spare them now. Danny, watching the sacrifice, was amazed at the lack of pity he felt for the dog. In spite of himself, he was being swept into the ways of his captors. Another great yell rose from the throats of the painted Chippewa. Without thinking, Danny joined in the cry. Indians, voyageurs, they were merely men fighting the terrible Manitou who threatened their frail canoes.

The humpbacked island showed itself clearly by late afternoon. Danny felt a strange growing excitement as they drew in close under white cliffs. The wild keening of the women for their dead was around him now, caught up by all of the women in the canoes, echoing weirdly across the water as they came into the place of the Indian dead.

The canoes rode straight toward the beach. Just before they touched, Danny flung himself out of it and into the water. This time he kept his feet. He had reached the ·Island of the Great Turtle.

Indian Life

THE VILLAGE was soon in order. Old women, their
gray hair stringing down their bent backs, had
gone quickly to work, screeching at the dogs and
raising the bark over the frames of their houses. Half-
naked children scampered about the settlement, playing
games and shouting with laughter, while the young men
who were not warriors practiced their marksmanship or
went hunting. Old men and warriors sat in front of their
fires, smoking and talking about the possibility of an
attack by the English.

Danny tried daily to reassure Sawaquot, hoping to
keep him and the tribe peaceable and unprepared if an
attack should occur; but as the days passed, he knew
deep in his heart that the attack would never come. Detroit could spare no soldiers. It was only from Niagara
that help could come, and that was doubtful. He wondered if Captain Etherington were still alive, and if he
had been able to send word of the massacre. Danny, his
days and nights spent now in an Indian lodge, kept hoping that help would come. Weeks passed. The Chippewa
lived in a constant fear of attack. Guards were everywhere. Still no word of an avenging army.

Danny, forbidden to leave the camp, realized that

escape from the island was impossible. Little by little, he began to adjust to his new life.

Hardly a day passed but what canoes came to the island with the red war hatchet of Pontiac in the hands of the messengers. They came to urge Sawaquot to join in the siege of Detroit. But the chief refused to let his young men go. Danny was grateful, and the coming of the canoes also gave him hope. If the Indians needed reinforcements, Detroit was still holding out successfully. Messengers came and left. The pines on the white cliffs were black now. Behind them the red of maples and the brilliant yellow of birches proclaimed September. Danny was still a prisoner.

He began to wonder if he would ever be free again. True, the family of the chief had shown him every kindness. There were five of them, Wah-bu-noong, the mother, Bah-we-tig, Woman of the Rapids, and her husband, Wah-be-a-tik, or White Elk. It was he whom Danny had seen on the first day of his arrival at the fort. It had been White Elk who had received the silver bracelets. Danny was glad now that he had added them to the trade goods that afternoon. White Elk still wore them proudly and it was White Elk and his son, Geb-wah-nuh-sins, Little Hawk, who taught him Chippewa. Little Hawk was about nine years old, Danny judged. His small sister, who had no name, followed Danny everywhere he went. Almost in spite of himself, Danny O'Hara began to become Misquah, the Chippewa. He hunted with the men, shared what they had.

Many times, when food was scarce, they found themselves forced to go for days at a time with hardly a mouthful to eat. During these days Danny joined with the others in painting his face with charcoal. Indianlike, they still showed the same cheerfulness as they had shown in the midst of plenty. A trip to one of the neighboring islands usually ended the fast for a time when they returned with fish or wildfowl.

It was at the end of one of these hunts that they felt the first flakes of snow on their faces. As they entered the lodge, the sun burst through the clouds and flooded the island in warm light.

Danny spoke in halting Chippewa. "Do you think the English will come?"

Fork-in-the-Tree said nothing for a moment. Finally he knocked the ashes from his pipe and turned to Danny.

"My son," he said, "you have been with us now for four moons. You are as one of Sawaquot's family. Little Hawk and his father, even Little Sister, think of you not as our captive, but as our brother. It pains Sawaquot to see this restlessness in you, and yet he understands. You have told how your father waits at the fort to the south. Be patient, my son. The English will come, but not for a while. Our White Father is powerful. You have seen my medal which the great chief of the white man gave to me. I know the strength of the English and the power of their fire sticks. Now we go south. It is our custom to spend the winters in small family groups. Thus the food is more plentiful. When the gray goose returns to his home in the north, we too gather again in the Moon of Maple Sugaring at the maple woods near Michilimackinac, south of L'Arbre Croche, the Crooked Tree, where stand the lodges of our brothers the Ottawa. It is then the English will come. You must wait until then."

The chief paused.

"But Fork-in-the-Tree," Danny's voice was pleading, "why could I not go on from your winter camp—on down the shore to Detroit? I could hide during the day and travel only at night."

The chief shook his head. "You would not go two marches, Misquah. Even in winter the woods are full of my people and of others. And do not think that your dress of a Chippewa would protect you. The tribes who follow Pontiac grow angry. They call us old women for not taking up the hatchet. If they found you alone in the forest, your red hair would soon hang at their belt."

"Don't go, Misquah," Little Hawk said. "You stay with us. My grandfather speaks the truth."

"Hear my father, Red-haired One." This time it was White Elk who spoke. "My father is wise. But for him you would long since have died beneath the hatchet. Let us eat and forget this talk."

Danny said nothing more. But in the back of his mind a plan still lingered. He wanted to ask where the wintering grounds were, but he knew it might give away his thoughts. If only they moved down the east side of the coast. They were now nearly three hundred miles from Detroit, but the wintering grounds might bring him closer. With a stolen canoe he could follow the shore south to the fort.

Little Sister came forward then with the bowls of food. While Danny ate, he tried to remember the route Jacques had taken from Detroit. But Little Sister kept jabbering to him in Chippewa. Finally Danny gave up. He would have plenty of time to think during the trip to the hunting grounds.

Two days later the canoes left for the south. The trip across the Straits of Mackinac was made quickly to avoid the "Old Woman of the Wind." They reached the Ottawa village of the Crooked Tree late in the afternoon. Most of the tribe remained, but Sawaquot, fearing for Danny's safety among the Ottawa, pushed on. It was then that Danny realized the truth of the chief's words. They were following the shores of Lake Michigan. Escape would be impossible until spring. When they made camp that night, Detroit had never seemed farther away.

Lost

Dawn was just coming through the trees when Sawaquot and the others again lifted packs to their shoulders. They pointed at Danny, still drowsily making his pack, and laughingly called him the sleepy one.

Danny tightened his belt glumly. Another morning without food. Shouldering his pack, he set off after the others.

The women, as usual, carried the largest packs, but they carried them without a murmur. Danny hurried past them to catch up with Little Hawk. He told Danny they were going farther inland to find game.

They walked twenty miles that day. Danny, after wolfing down his portion of dried corn and fat, was glad to rest in the hastily erected shelter the women put up.

Sometime later, White Elk came into the wigwam and said that he had killed a doe. The next morning they would move the lodge to the carcass.

The doe, Danny found the next morning, was not far away. Again the lodge was put up and the kettle set to boil. That afternoon they ate their fill. While the men lounged about the fire, the women finished cutting the venison into strips. These were hung in the smoke to dry.

Lying there, Danny began to feel restless. The men were snoring loudly; even Little Hawk was asleep. Danny got to his feet and stretched. He decided that he would take a short walk into the woods. Taking his musket, Danny left the campfire.

Bah-we-tig looked up as he passed.

"I go for fresh meat," Danny said, smiling.

White Elk's wife nodded and went back to tend the smoking venison.

When he was out of sight, Danny halted. The sun was bright above the trees, and Danny took a deep breath. This was the first time since his captivity that he had been completely alone. Danny started on. The tracks of a rabbit crossed his path. Danny followed them for a little ways, marking where they crossed over logs and around tall trees. The tracks disappeared. Danny wandered on, enjoying his new-found freedom.

It wasn't until he was deep in the woods that he thought of escaping. The thought made his heart pound. He paused, looked around him. He knew about where they were. He had his musket, powder, and ball. Why hadn't he thought to fill a pouch with corn and dried venison? Would he ever stop being a greenhorn? he wondered.

Danny glanced up at the sun. It was low over the trees and the winter night was not too far off. What would happen if he didn't return? Sawaquot would probably wait until morning before he started searching; by then, Danny thought, he could be hours away. Still, tracking him in the snow would be easy. Danny sat down on a blasted pine stump to think. He had to escape, but how?

Looking up at the darkening woods, he knew now that being a true "man of the North" was more than knowing how to paddle a canoe or shoot a gun. Except for his brief hunting trips at Detroit and at Michilimackinac, he had never been on his own in the woods, at least not in forests such as these. Always before there had been familiar landmarks to guide him. He wondered what Jacques would have done. Probably pick a tree ahead and walk to it to keep from going in circles, then on to another and another. Perhaps even climbing a tree now and then to scan the country. If he only had a map! The only map he had ever seen had belonged to Jacques. Then there was food. Even if he were lucky and found squirrel or porcupine or even a deer, he would be able to pack only a little with him. Thinking back to the times he had pretended that he had been a voyageur, Danny felt a sense of shame. What a little boy he had been. His time for play acting was over now, and his time for escape, Danny realized, had gone by. If he had only taken a canoe before the rivers had frozen, he might have reached Detroit long ago. And what if he had reached Detroit? Would he have found it still defended or would he have found a pile of charred timbers, his mother and father dead or captives?

Danny jumped to his feet. There was no point in sitting there thinking of what might have happened. That was childish. There was only one thing to do: go back to the camp and wait until the rivers opened. Then he would steal a canoe and head for Detroit. Next time he would be sure and take provisions. There was no other way. Suddenly Danny realized that the sun had dropped out of sight. He began to hurry, following the tracks he had made. The woods grew darker. He broke into a trot, then slowed as he saw his tracks growing dim in the coming darkness. A light snow began to fall. Danny stopped to catch his breath. All around him huge trees reared up in a wall of rough bark. An owl hooted just above his head. Danny jumped. A twig broke. It sounded like a musket shot in the sharp cold.

The snow drifted down in huge flakes now, and was shutting out the sky. He was lost! Danny opened his mouth to shout, but he let the sound die in his throat. There might be other Indians near—unfriendly Indians.

Danny leaned his gun against a tree and began to swing his arms to keep warm. Still he wasn't afraid— when morning came he could find his way back. The main thing was to keep calm and as warm as possible. Taking his hatchet from under his blanket, he began tearing the bark from a large birch close at hand. First he made a deep cut down the side of the tree, then carefully he pulled the bark from the trunk, peeling it down until he had a piece large enough. He laid it flat on the ground, weighted it down with some chunks of dead wood, then began to gather twigs for a fire. Kneeling, he set the tinder aflame with the lock of his musket. When the fire was burning brightly, he lay down on the birch mat after brushing the snow from the white bark, and covered himself with his blanket. The fire crackled cheerfully, and he slept.

Danny awoke three times to add wood to the fire. Each time he looked at the dark sky, and each time he heard wolves.

Toward morning he was unable to go back to sleep. He sat hugging his knees till dawn. It had stopped snowing, but the heavy gray sky still hid the sun. Danny looked at the clouds in disgust. He rewrapped the lock of his musket in its piece of deerskin and started through the trees. The camp couldn't be too far off.

Twice he stumbled over hidden branches. The snow was deeper than it had been the night before, and once he fell full length in a drift. He struggled to his feet, brushed the snow from his gun, and stumbled on. The trees began to look familiar. Danny quickened his pace only to stop in dismay—straight ahead stood a stripped birch and the ashes of a campfire. He had made a complete circle.

Fear touched him. He started off again, only to stumble and fall. This time he noticed that it was harder to rise. Bitterly he wished that he had never left camp. At least he should have thought to bring some of the drying venison.

He kept moving along what he hoped was his trail. The sight of the stripped birch had shaken him, and he kept bearing left, hoping to avoid his previous mistake. Branches tore at his blanket or snatched stubbornly at the strap of his pouch and powder horn. Once he was forced to stop to loosen his leggings from a brier bush; and when he turned to go on, a root sent him sprawling in the snow. He lay there for a moment to rest. The urge to lie still was very strong, but he tried to fight himself to his feet. Lying in the snow was certain death—he knew that, but still he lay there.

A sudden crashing in the underbrush brought him

The huge animal snorted

upright. Danny snatched the cover from his musket. Slowly the branches ahead parted, sending down a shower of snow. A huge rack of antlers thrust itself through the opening. Not the antlers of a deer—these were more like wide-pointed baskets.

The antlers moved closer, followed by a mammoth head with a pendulous lower lip and an immense nose with flaring nostrils. Danny was face to face with a giant moose!

He raised his gun. The huge animal snorted! Danny pulled the trigger. There was a sharp report, and the moose whirled and lunged back into the thicket. Danny caught a glimpse of the wide hindquarters. The right hind leg was dragging, and the hair was furrowed with red gashes.

He fumbled for his powder horn. The animal was wounded and wouldn't move too fast. Besides, those were the marks of wolves on the hindquarters, probably the very wolves he had heard in the night.

Danny's fingers closed about a broken strap. Frantically he looked at his belt—his powder horn was gone, torn off by a broken branch. It was then that the fear and the hunger drove Danny almost mad. Clutching his now useless gun, Danny plunged crazily after the retreating animal, forgetting the danger from a wounded moose in his wild rush after the only thing that could save him—fresh meat.

Trees thrust him this way and that. His breath was coming in great tearing sobs, his chest heaving, burning in the cold that frosted his nostrils. Twice he saw patches of fresh blood. The woods grew darker. Danny wallowed on, falling, gasping. A branch tore his gun from his hand. On his knees, Danny tugged at the heavy musket. Sobbing with exhaustion, he made it to his feet. Danny took one step forward. The woods seemed to explode as a great hoof crashed against Danny's forehead. He pitched into the snow.

Fighting unconsciousness, Danny raised his head. Something sticky and warm was in his eyes. Danny lifted one hand and dabbed at his face. The hand was dark when he brought it down, but he could see.

Something was moving in front of him. Danny got to his knees. The wounded moose, muzzle resting on the ground, raised his foreleg again. The sharp hoof pawed at Danny.

Somehow the boy found his knife. He held it in both hands, raising his arms with his last bit of strength. Danny was blind again, but he drove the knife down with all his might.

Black Bear Medicine

FORK-IN-THE-TREE, White Elk, and Little Hawk had started out to search for Danny. They looked all day and had even gone to the lodge of a medicine man eight miles to the north to ask if he had seen the boy. He had seen nothing, and the new snow had covered any trail, so that on the evening of the second day the men had returned to camp. Sawaquot had gone mournfully into his lodge, when from the west had come the faint crack of a musket. As one man, the three Indians whirled and darted back into the woods.

They were walking silently, looking for "sign," when suddenly White Elk let out a cry. Hanging on a stump was Danny's powder horn.

They found the trail then, a wavering, crazy stumble of tracks spotted with blood. Twice Sawaquot knelt and sniffed at the spoor like a hound, then they sped on over the frantic trail.

Little Hawk was the first to see the moose. He ran forward, calling to the others who were moving like shadows among the trees; they stopped, staring. The immense rack of horns flared upward from a welter of broken brush, and the giant brown body lay sprawled in the snow like an old crumpled blanket. Spread-eagled, half on top and half in front of the dead moose, lay the still form of Danny. One arm was twisted under him, the other still grasped the knife which was plunged to the hilt in the neck of the moose. Blood was everywhere, tinting the snow a bright pink. But the moose had saved Danny's life, for the warm, furry body had kept him from freezing.

Sawaquot spoke a sharp word of command. Little Hawk turned and raced back along the trail while the other two set about making a rough litter.

It was pitch-dark by the time they reached camp. The swaying, blanket-wrapped figure of Danny hung between the two poles of the litter.

Quickly the women built a roaring fire in the lodge. Soon Danny lay on a pile of skins, stripped to his breechclout. His eyes were closed, and the gaping red gash in his forehead was like an open mouth.

Danny opened his eyes to the "chuck, chuck" of a rattle. A face livid with red and white paint was close to his own, a face half covered with the head and pelt of a wolf. Danny shuddered and tried to rise, but the pain in his head drove him back onto the couch. The face swam in a sort of mist. A hand was at his mouth, forcing his lips apart.

"Drink," grunted the face.

A scalding liquid, nauseous and bitter, flooded Danny's throat. He gulped and swallowed. The rattle began again.

Face burning with fever, Danny was dimly conscious of shadows moving above him. A weird chant came from the lips of the medicine man. The song rose and fell;

the rattles clicked; a drum began to beat. Danny felt himself sinking—sinking.

It was three days later when Danny regained consciousness. A cold winter's sun made a yellow circle in the lodge roof. He raised his hand to his head—the wound was closed.

"Where is the moose?" Danny spoke aloud. There was no answer. Danny sat up. The lodge was empty. Delicious cooking smells came from the steaming pot in the center of the wigwam. Slowly Danny threw back the bearskin that covered him and got to his knees. Then he was standing on wobbly legs, moving toward the kettle.

A sudden draft of cold air struck his bare back. Light flooded the lodge. Danny turned his head.

"Misquah is better?" It was the chief's daughter, Bah-we-tig.

"I am well," Danny said. His voice seemed to be coming from someone else. "And I am hungry," he added.

"Meno. Good!" She came into the lodge and bent down over Danny's bed. When she straightened, Danny saw that she was holding his shirt and leggings. He managed to keep his feet until he finished dressing, then he walked carefully back to his sleeping furs and sat down.

Bah-we-tig began filling a birch bowl with food. Danny thought she would never finish. As she came toward him he reached up and almost snatched the bowl from her hands. He finished the food quickly, eating in noisy gulps, and begged for more. Bah-we-tig shook her head. "Later," she said.

After she had gone out again, Danny lay back on the furs. Strength was coming back into his arms and legs.

Danny sat up. His musket stood in one corner of the wigwam. He slipped on moccasins, got to his feet, and wrapped himself in a blanket. Then, leaning on his musket, made his way out of the dark wigwam.

The light on the snow almost blinded him. Danny shaded his eyes with one hand and blinked. Bah-we-tig and Wah-bu-noong were on their knees in the snow, working on a huge brown shape between them. Danny hobbled closer. They were busily scraping flesh from a stretched skin. Little Sister was watching them, a cornstalk doll tight in her arms.

"Moose?" Danny pointed to the skin.

"Yours," the young woman said and smiled at Danny.

So he had killed the moose after all. Danny took a deep breath of the crisp air. "Where are the men?" he asked.

The women pointed toward the woods.

Danny nodded. Squatting down beside the wigwam, he watched the women work. Little Sister came toward him, holding out her doll.

"Broken," she said. "Misquah make new one for Little Sister?"

"I don't know," Danny said. He wished the men would return. He was anxious to learn what had happened after he had stabbed the moose.

"You make white man's doll?" Little Sister squatted down beside him, her black braids almost touching Danny's knees as she looked up into his face.

Danny gave in. The small child reminded him strangely of someone else. Her round eyes were more brown than black, and her small pointed face was pale copper under the smudges.

"Get me small pine log, so big," Danny said. Little Sister jumped up and scurried over to the small pile of firewood that lay to one side of the clearing. Danny pulled his knife from its beaded sheath. He realized suddenly how much he had missed talking to a woman. Wah-bu-noong and her daughter were silent when the men were about, jabbering to each other only when there were other women near or when they were working. When they spoke to Danny it was always in one or two short words.

Little Sister came back from the woodpile, dragging a huge length of log. Danny grinned and rose to his feet to help her. The women looked up from their scraping. Danny took the log from the child's arms, broke off a short length of limb, and went back to the door of the wigwam. He reached inside the flap and pulled out a bearskin. Spreading it on the ground, Danny sat down and motioned for Little Sister to sit beside him.

The women took up their work again, the younger chattering to her mother in a low voice and smiling. Danny couldn't make out what they were saying, but he knew from the expression on Wah-bu-noong's face that she was pleased to see him playing with her granddaughter.

Danny began peeling the rough bark from the limb.

Little Sister, watching him, said in Chippewa, "Where do you live?"

"Do you mean where is my home?"

"You speak Chippewa, not French. Why do you speak Chippewa, Misquah?"

"Because I am Frenchman and wish to learn." Danny

looked closely at the child to see if she doubted him. If he told her the truth, she might forget and tell his secret. Then all of his plans for escape in the spring would be spoiled.

The child nodded her head. "You tell me where is your house."

"Far to the south," Danny said.

"What are you carving?"

Danny held up the peeled stick. "This," he said, "is going to be the head." He pointed to the two notches he had made for a neck.

"Where are her eyes?"

"They will be here, so," Danny said. He took the point of his knife and dug out two small holes.

"Will she be Indian doll?" Little Sister's small head was close to his hands.

Danny pushed her gently back. "This knife is sharp," he warned. "Little Sister must sit down or she will hurt herself."

The child moved quickly, squatting back on her haunches.

"Make me French doll," she said.

Danny scowled. This was getting more difficult. The thick-bladed hunting knife, sharp as it was, lacked the point to do any careful cutting. He had planned to make just the eyes and mouth and maybe paint the face.

"Wouldn't you rather have a nice Indian doll?" Danny asked hopefully.

Little Sister shook her head firmly. "French doll with very pretty dress," she said.

Danny stopped carving to think. Somewhere he had a handkerchief that Pierre had given him. "Wait here," he said and went inside the lodge. When he came out again, he had a bright blue handkerchief in his hands. It was wrinkled but clean, and when the child saw the colored cloth with the small yellow flowers, her eyes grew bright with happiness.

Danny set to work eagerly. The making of a white man's doll was becoming suddenly important. Just as if the crudely carved figure taking shape in his hands were really coming alive.

He finished the head and body. No use making feet, he decided. The kerchief dress would cover them. The arms puzzled him at first. Finally he took two small strips of bark from the lodge wall, rolled them, cut them evenly, and glued them to the body with spruce gum. The hair he took from the bearskin, fastening it to the head with balsam also. All he needed was paint for the face. Danny dug into his pouch and came up with two pots of face paint. With a sharp stick he carefully touched the mouth and nose with red, then drew in eyes and eyebrows with the black. He wished he could have made the eyes blue. He tried to remember what blue eyes looked like, and couldn't. It bothered him.

Little Sister was tugging on his sleeve. She held the blue sprigged kerchief.

Danny frowned. How was he going to make a dress? Bah-we-tig could make one, but he wanted to complete the doll himself. Danny had an idea. He laid the kerchief on the ground, folded it in half, and cut a small square out of the center. Then he pulled it over the doll's head.

Another strand of red wool for a belt, and the doll was finished. He handed it to Little Sister.

With a squeal of delight she cradled the new doll tight against her stained deerskin dress. "Pretty," she said, "pretty." Little Sister began to croon softly, rocking the small doll in her arms. Suddenly she looked up at Danny, her small face filled with admiration. Danny turned away.

"What is her name?" Little Sister asked.

Danny was slipping his knife back into his beaded sheath. "Call her Annette," he said.

The child nodded solemnly, then she ran toward her mother.

At dusk the hunters returned. They showed no surprise at Danny's being on his feet, but Danny knew they were glad. Inside the lodge they told Danny about the moose and how the medicine man had been brought to cure him.

That night, after a delicious meal of moose, Danny gave the hide to Sawaquot.

"In the name of my family, I thank you," the chief said. "We will make a huge vat for maple sugaring when the time comes."

"We thank you for the doll." White Elk spoke up from the doorway. "Little Sister is grateful. You shall have much maple sugar at the village of the Crooked Tree."

"It is nothing," Danny said. But he was thinking, "When maple sugaring comes, I will be on my way to Detroit." Somehow the words lacked their usual strength. With the family of Sawaquot around him, he felt at peace for the first time since his captivity.

In a week Danny felt strong enough to hunt again. His musket was clean and shining, but it seemed strangely heavy to him as he joined the others one morning. At first he thought he would leave it behind. His powder was running low, and Little Hawk could bring down any small game with his bow. Sawaquot carried a musket, White Elk bow and hunting arrows. Danny hesitated. Should he leave his gun behind or not? He realized suddenly that he hesitated not because of the light powder horn, but because of the fear of meeting another moose.

The men were almost out of sight. Danny looked back at the lodge. Smoke curled from the top of the rounded roof. It looked unusually inviting. Danny's hand tightened on the musket, then he was hurrying down the trail after the hunters.

The four of them spread out in a single line, moving quietly under snow-laden branches. There had been a thaw only a few days before, but now the woods were white with new-fallen snow. Ahead of them, through bare trees, Danny saw a lake, gray-white under its coat of ice.

"Mahgwah!" Little Hawk let out a shout.

Danny and the others ran over to where he was standing. Above him reared a dead pine. Near the top was a dark hole.

"What is it you say, Geb-wah-nuh-sins?" Danny asked excitedly.

"Look, Misquah." Little Hawk touched the trunk of the tree. Great gashes scored the rough bark. Claw marks.

"Mahgwah. Bear," White Elk said. "He is holed up. See, there are no tracks in the snow."

"You have made a good find, Grandson," Sawaquot said. "Run now to camp. Tell the women we have found the mahgwah. Bring our axes."

"I go." Little Hawk sped off.

White Elk and Fork-in-the-Tree were walking around and around the pine. They stopped, said something to each other in a low tone, and looked at Danny. Danny wondered how they would get the bear out of the tree.

White Elk came forward. "We have decided, Misquah, that you shall have the honor of shooting the great bear. It is right that our brother should have his own bear-skin."

Danny's heart began to beat faster. He was remembering the moose. He wanted to refuse, but White Elk and the chief were watching him closely. Danny's hands against the cold steel of his gun felt damp. How would a bear act when he came out of a tree?

"I will shoot the bear, Wah-be-a-tik."

The Chippewa smiled. "Shoot well, Misquah," he said.

"It is good," Sawaquot added. "Misquah has need for a bear."

Danny wondered if they knew how scared he was. When that bear was awakened and came down out of his snug tree, he would be angry. And from the height of the claw marks, the bear must be a big one. To cover his thoughts, Danny began readying his gun. He had trouble removing the deerskin cover. His hands shook slightly as he made sure the powder was dry in the pan.

Behind him he heard the crack of a twig. Little Hawk

strode into the clearing. With him came the women. They were carrying axes.

Danny put his musket at half cock and leaned it against a tree. They took turns chopping at the base of the tall pine. It was as thick as two men at the butt, and soon the snow was littered with yellow chips. Danny handed his ax to White Elk. The tree was tottering. He snatched up his musket.

The pine started downward. White Elk jumped clear. At the edge of the clearing, he fitted an arrow to his bow. The pine came down with a crash. Danny brought the hammer on his flintlock into full cock.

Something huge and black was coming out of the fallen tree. The bear lowered his head, blinking angrily in the sunlight. Danny raised his musket. The long head with its brownish snout swung slowly toward him. Still Danny held his fire. Growling deep in his throat, the animal started toward him. On it came in a shuffling lope, surprising in its swiftness. Danny remained motionless, the musket leveled. The bear was almost on him, but Danny, staring at the huge black muzzle, saw instead the branching horns of a moose. Dimly he heard someone shouting. There was a blinding flash. Danny stepped backward, tripped, and sat down heavily in the snow.

The smell of powder was sharp in his nostrils. Something heavy and black lay across his outstretched legs.

"Misquah shoots well." Little Hawk came running up to him. He danced around the dead bear, waving his bow.

Danny pulled his legs from beneath the huge animal and got to his feet. His musket was covered with snow.

Danny brushed it clean. His hand found his powder horn. As he poured the black grains into the muzzle, he was thinking of the charging bear that had turned into a moose. Where would he be now if someone hadn't shouted for him to shoot?

He looked at the red-skinned faces around him. Savages? Perhaps, but no one could ask for truer friends. They had saved him from the massacre, saved him from the woods, and now they had saved him from himself. Red men or white, people needed each other.

White Elk was smiling. "Big bear," he said. "Plenty of meat now."

Danny grinned. He had killed his first bear.

The two women were kneeling by the fallen bear. To Danny's surprise, he heard them asking the bear's forgiveness.

"Oh, grandfather," they wailed, "please forgive us for killing you. Forgive our brother Misquah. We need food, oh bear." The skinning knives began to flash.

Danny felt a sudden stir of sympathy for the bear lying so still. Without knowing it, right at that moment, Danny O'Hara was very close to becoming an Indian.

He felt a tug on his leggings. It was Little Sister. "Misquah is great hunter," she said.

Danny saw the crude French doll in her arms and his face changed. He wondered how long it would be until the Moon of Maple Sugaring.

Back at the lodge the bear's head was placed on the ground and the men set about building a scaffold of limbs. Danny took his ax and helped them. Soon the platform was finished, and the black, furry head was lifted up onto it. Sawaquot removed his silver bracelets and hung them over the bear's ears, and the others followed suit, draping necklaces of wampum and gewgaws over the head. Danny pulled off his own ornaments and laid them next to the others. Sawaquot looked at him with approval as he took several twists of tobacco from his pouch and placed them carefully under the bear's nose.

It was dark when they finished the preparations. After a hearty meal from Danny's moose, the family lay down to sleep.

Danny awoke to the sound of sweeping. The women were busy clearing the ground in front of the lodge. Danny stepped out into the morning and seated himself next to the men who were squatting in front of their mirrors, busily painting their faces. He took his own mirror from his belt and began to mix his paint. Carefully he traced a design in red and black on his face, trying to imitate that used by the chief.

Their faces painted at last, the four of them strode to the bear's head. A new stroud blanket was unfolded and laid under the head, with many apologies for disturbing his rest. Then Fork-in-the-Tree filled his pipe, lighted it, and began to blow smoke into the bear's nostrils. He handed the pipe to Danny who drew in a mouthful of smoke, let it trickle toward the black, furry lump, then passed it on to White Elk. Little Hawk followed suit, and the feast was ready to begin.

They sat side by side in the lodge while the chief called once more on the spirits of the dead and upon the spirit of the dead bear.

The voice ceased and Danny came back with a start to

the scurrying sound of moccasins. The women were
dragging their kettles from the lodge and kindling a fire.
Danny lay back sniffing the air for the first smell of
cooking meat, letting the fire melt the cold from his
cramped muscles.

The bear meat was delicious. Danny and the others
ate all they could hold, then lay curled up in their

blankets, enjoying the new warmth in the clear air. There was a softness in the breeze that told them that it was time to be moving back to the shore where they had left their canoes, then back to the Island of the Great Turtle. The Moon of the Crusted Snow was long since gone. Now they would have to carry all of their meat and skins and camping equipment on their backs for thirty miles. Sawaquot had told Danny that they had nearly four hundred-weight of bear meat alone, plus the moose. Then there were the pelts.

Danny sat bolt upright. This was the season for trading furs at the fort. He wondered if they would let him see Pierre and Ahwun and Annette. He made up his mind to ask the chief as soon as he could. Instead of making his escape at the village of the Crooked Tree, he would wait until they reached the fort. A week wouldn't make any difference, and it would be easier to escape with Pierre's help. Besides, he had a bearskin and a share of the beaver pelts to sell.

Maple Sugar and the Fort

THEY STARTED back, two days later. Sawaquot said they would stop at Crooked Tree long enough for sugar making, then on to Michilimackinac. Danny was filled with impatience. Even the hardships of the march failed to lessen his excitement, and his new strength seemed limitless. For days he led the others, carrying backbreaking loads that would have tired even Jacques.

They marched all day, every day. At daybreak they were off, walking till late afternoon. After building a rough platform to protect their goods from wolves, they would hurry back for a second load. From scaffold to scaffold they marched, through rain which beat their faces and turned the trails into rivers of mud, then froze into ruts until the trail became a staggering horror. Danny spoke little now. His face grew thin, and the scar on his forehead was an angry red. In the dark shadows beneath his brows, his blue eyes were bright and a little wild. Then one day they reached their canoe, hidden on the shore of Lake Michigan. Two days later they were at the village of the Ottawa. Maple-sugaring time was at hand.

But as the sugar making drew toward a close, the camp began to lose some of its gaiety. A constant watch now was kept, for fear the English would come seeking vengeance for the massacre. Danny, walking among the groups of warriors, was conscious of whispers and dark looks. Even Sawaquot was worried. The old women in the camp awoke daily to tell of their dreams of the avenging English.

The camp grew hostile. Danny was forced to stay close to Sawaquot and his family. Tempers flared. The old fears that had lain quiet through the winter began to come back to Danny. So it was with a sense of relief that Danny, one morning, saw the canoes being loaded for their departure. The morning was quiet—hardly a leaf moved. The broad blue lake was pond-still, with only a narrow line of waves reaching up on the sand. It looked sleepy, like a person awaking from a long nap.

Danny dipped his paddle. Their loaded canoe swung into line with the others heading for the village of the Crooked Tree. They planned to spend the night there, then push on toward the fort. Danny yearned for some new clothes. Those he wore were torn and dirty. He knew he smelled like an Indian—the village dogs had long since ceased barking at him—but he wondered about buying clothing. He felt as though he could never go back to the old store. Even if the Indians had not broken in, to go back after clothes was out of the question. He decided he would take his pelts and trade elsewhere in the fort.

As he watched the foaming wake of the canoe, the pain of Jacques' death welled up again inside. Less than a year before he had watched this same lake, praying for the sight of just such a wake coming from the bobbing canoe of his dead friend. Jacques would paddle no more, unless it was in the next world. Danny hoped that the legends of the Chippewa were true. They seemed to suit Jacques somehow, more closely than the hereafter the priest at home had talked about. To the Chippewa, the hereafter meant traveling to a distant land where those who were good found a wonderful country filled with deer and moose and bear, where all the animals of the land and air and water joined with the fruit of the ground to provide feasting and luxury. Jacques would be happy there, Danny knew, with a canoe and his gun and his beloved lakes and forests.

The sound of paddles filled Danny's mind with peace; and for the first time in many months, he began to sing. It was the song of the Young Voyageur. The listening Indians dipped their paddles faster. The canoes sped on.

Danny forgot where he was in the rhythm of the dipping paddles. It was a new fresh world of warm blue sky and sparkling water. He finished his song, letting his voice soar on the "joy in the heart," and began another. It was the song he hadn't sung since he had left home; and as Danny sang the familiar words, it seemed as though it was not Sawaquot guiding the canoe, but Jacques.

"*Alouette, gentille alouette,*" he sang. "Little skylark, pretty little skylark."

A herring gull, white wings flashing, hovered over Danny's head for a moment, then slid away to dive into the water. He came up with a squirming fish in his beak and rose high into the air. Danny followed the bird with his eyes till it was a small speck on the horizon. The village of L'Arbre Croche was in sight.

They set out from L'Arbre Croche the next morning with the others and on again toward the fort. The Ottawas had told them that all was peaceful, and the Chippewa paddled with more confidence. They camped that night; and on the third day they saw the familiar palisades of Fort Michilimackinac.

Danny paused and held up his paddle across the thwarts, scanning the shore for the white speck that would be the cabin of Pierre. He saw it at last, nestled deep in the trees. He wasn't sure, but he thought he saw a flash of scarlet at the door. Danny drove his paddle down with such force that the canoe swung sharply to one side, and the others had to paddle quickly to keep the heavily laden canoe from capsizing.

"Mah-na-dud! Bad!" Sawaquot's voice was stern. "It is not good, Misquah, to upset us. Our canoe has brought us safe to our homes. Use care that you do not cause us to lose that for which we have worked."

"I am sorry, but I thought I saw the red cap of Pierre." Danny hadn't meant to give way to his excitement, but the flash of red had been too much for him.

"Be patient, my brother." Sawaquot spoke kindly. "We shall first pay our debts and buy what we need, then you may go to visit Pierre and my sister."

Danny's heart sang as he saw the beach approaching. How kind Sawaquot was to let him go, if only for a few hours.

The canoe drove hard onto the beach, and Danny leaped out to pull it to safety. One by one the other canoes drew alongside, and soon a long procession started up the trail toward the fort. Danny had just swung his pelts to his shoulder when a familiar voice spoke to him in Chippewa.

"Ah, Misquah, you have returned at last."

Danny dropped his bundle and whirled to see Old Pierre standing at his side.

"Pierre." Danny seized the old man in a bear hug. He was amazed at how small Pierre seemed. "How are Maman and Annette?"

"They are well and asking for you. You will stay with us, no?"

"Sawaquot says I may come as soon as we unload. I want to get some new clothes; and, Pierre, do you have any hot water for a bath?"

"Of course!" Pierre chuckled. "I go now to tell them that you are home."

"Good! I will be there soon, Pierre." He watched the old man hurry off, thinking how good it would be to wear clean clothes again and hear French spoken instead of Chippewa.

When Danny came out of the trading post (he had avoided going near the shuttered store that had been Jacques'), Danny was poorer by thirty-five pounds of beaver. But he had a new pair of leggings, two shirts, a new coat, and ammunition. He carried them in a bundle with the bearskin and a bolt of blue-and-white-checked cloth. The cloth was for Annette. The bearskin he planned to give to Pierre and Maman.

As he hurried toward Pierre's, Danny saw a canoe full of warriors heading for the shore. More messengers from Pontiac, he thought. According to the wampum they carried, they were still seeking recruits for Pontiac.

Detroit, then, was holding out and Danny hurried on filled with new hope.

Holding the bearskin bundle in front of him, Danny knocked at Pierre's door. The door swung inward and Annette stood smiling up at him. For a moment Danny felt as though his heart would burst inside. Her long braids shone like crow's wings and her small face was filled with happiness.

"Danny!" Pierre came hurrying past her, his face alight. Maman stood smiling in the kitchen. "Welcome, welcome! We thought you were never coming. Here, let me take your things before you drop them. Look, Maman, at Danny's head. He has hurt himself. Annette, is the water boiling?" Pierre was almost shouting in his excitement. "Fill the big tub in the kitchen, Annette.

Then stay with your maman until we are finished. This Indian . . . whew!" Pierre held his nose with his fingers.

Danny dropped his bundle in Pierre's hands and fled into the kitchen. He could hardly wait for that hot water and new clothes.

The rough walls of the kitchen were hazy with steam from the wide wooden tub that stood in front of the fireplace. Glancing about him, Danny was surprised at the smallness of the room. Even the roof seemed much lower than he had remembered. He began to undress quickly while Pierre talked in a steady stream about the conditions at the fort. He had been able to keep the Indians out of the store, and Danny's things were still safe, as were Jacques'. He couldn't understand why Danny didn't want to go back now; after all, he must want his own belongings. But Danny shook his head. Pierre, shrugging his shoulders, let the matter drop.

Danny doubled up in the tub, letting the hot water seep clear through him. Some of it slopped over the sides and made puddles on the sand-scrubbed floor. Pierre only waved his hand and brought more. There was real soap too, made, as usual, from fat and ashes. It had a sharp, clean smell, reminding Danny of another kitchen where his mother used to have to force him to bathe; but Danny shut out these thoughts and began to scrub. He washed his hair last. Pierre, holding the huge black kettle, poured the steaming water over his red locks. While he stood drying in front of the fire, Pierre trimmed his hair. Danny felt as though he could breathe again.

The new breeches of scarlet cloth scratched his skin delightfully. Even the shirt, crackling new, sent little shivers of pleasure down his back. He slipped his feet into the new moccasins that he had been saving and stood up. Pierre was gazing at him with approval. Danny was improved—the awkward angles and bony wrists of a boy were gone. So was the smooth roundness of a young boy's face.

He must be well over six feet tall, thought Pierre, and his wide shoulders sloped powerfully under his shirt. A boy no longer, but a man. Daniel O'Hara, a woodsman with flaming red hair. His blue eyes gleamed as though he had never known death or captivity, and he wore the scar on his forehead like a badge of honor.

"Now!" Pierre was rubbing his hands together. "Now for some corn bread, real sweet potatoes, your tea, and"—he grinned—"beef!"

"Beef? Where in the world did you get beef?"

Pierre's face shone with pleasure. "From the Father at the village of L'Arbre Croche."

Danny rubbed his hand across his lean middle. "Let's eat," he said.

A Bit of Blue Ribbon

THE EVENING, and the days that followed, were like heaven to Danny O'Hara. After the first night, when he had been unable to sleep until he had pulled his blankets from his soft bed to sleep on the floor, he had begun to settle back into the comforts of civilization. The simple things of Pierre's house constantly amazed him. He had almost forgotten the taste of tea, and the solid roof over his head seemed strange after the open top of an Indian lodge.

Sawaquot visited him daily, and he told Danny to stay in the cabin. The Indians were coming from Detroit almost every day, looking for more warriors. Several had asked if there were any Englishmen about. They would kill them and make broth to give their brothers, the Chippewa, so that they would find courage to join Pontiac.

Danny decided he would wait a few days longer before trying his flight to the south.

But it was Annette's new dress that finally made Danny disregard Fork-in-the-Tree's warning.

Ahwun had been sewing diligently; and one afternoon Annette stood in front of Danny wearing the new gingham. He watched her, thinking how nice a pair of blue ribbons would look tied in her hair.

Danny made up his mind to get the ribbon. He was growing tired of staying indoors. Taking his musket and his last beaver pelt, he set off along the path. Annette begged him to take her along, but he refused. It was too dangerous, he said, and besides, she might soil her new dress. She stood in the door, watching his tall figure swing along the path toward the fort.

As Danny approached the gate he saw that a fresh band of messengers had arrived. Cradling his musket, he walked straight for them. They stood aside to let him pass. But no sooner was he through the gate than a sudden commotion at his back made him turn. A young brave, with three scalps at his side, left the group and came running toward him. Danny loosened the tomahawk in his belt and waited. The brave slid to a stop and stood looking at him uncertainly, fingering his war club.

"What does my red brother wish?" Danny spoke in Chippewa.

The Indian seemed undecided. He glanced over his shoulder to make sure that the others of his clan were still behind him.

"You are the redheaded Englishman of whom we have heard. Come with us now to our great chief Pontiac so that we may make broth of you to give the Chippewa courage. They are old women, the Chippewa, and refuse to join us." He raised his club threateningly, and his blanket fell from his shoulders. Danny saw another scalp at his belt. It had long blond hair, from which a bit of ribbon hung. It was the hair of a child.

The scar on Danny's forehead grew purple. The brave

rushed in, war club raised. Danny swung the butt of his musket upward and caught the scowling Indian in the face. The brave threw up his hands and staggered backward, the war club spinning from his fingers.

Danny, placing his foot on the fallen club, leveled his musket. A murmur arose among the band. They strained forward to look at their fallen comrade. He lay still, moaning a little. Blood poured from his nose.

Suddenly Sawaquot stood at Danny's side. He pushed Danny's musket barrel down and walked straight toward the glowering warriors. "This is our answer to your war hatchet. Our young men will not join you. We have just returned from hunting and we wish to go back to the Island of the Great Turtle in peace. Go back to your village! I, Sawaquot, chief of the Chippewa, have spoken."

Danny held his musket ready; if any raised his gun toward Fork-in-the-Tree, he would shoot him down. The warriors were muttering among themselves, and one half-raised his musket. Danny swung his barrel till it covered the breast of the angry Indian. There was no mistaking the look in his eyes. Slowly two of the warriors bent down, lifted the fallen brave, and dragged him toward their canoes. Danny's finger itched to pull the trigger. He could still see the blond scalp. Then they were gone, and in a moment the prow of their canoe passed the fort going south.

Sawaquot turned his head and stared at Danny. "You were foolish, my brother. Our neighbors, the Wyandotte, are angry and will seek your scalp. Some of our young men are undecided—they wish to join Pontiac—while others wish to go to Michilimackinac. It is not easy to hold a tribe together."

"But"—Danny was still angry—"he had the scalp of a child at his belt."

Sawaquot smiled grimly. "Do your soldiers then never kill our women and children?"

Danny looked down at the ground. He knew that it was true, but somehow it had seemed different when he had heard about an attack on an *Indian* village. Sawaquot loved his children too. Danny lifted his head. Fork-in-the-Tree was walking away toward his lodge.

Danny bought the blue ribbon and went back to Pierre's. But the more he thought about the fresh scalps he had seen, the more determined he was to go to Detroit. He was silent through supper. Annette, pretty in her new dress and ribbons, waited for him to say something to her. But Danny, eating slowly, seemed to have forgotten that she was in the room. At last he rose from his half-eaten food and strode to the door, where he stood looking out over the water. "Pierre," he said at last, "I must go to Detroit."

"So?" Pierre raised his eyebrows. "And how do you expect to do that?"

Danny shook his head and began to pace up and down the room.

"I am afraid that it is hopeless for now, Danny. Not until your king sends troops. You know yourself that Pontiac's army grows bigger and that Detroit has been long under siege. How can you or I go to their aid; and what good would two men do?"

Danny stopped pacing and faced Pierre. "I will buy

your canoe, Pierre. You may have my things at the store —anything you ask—but I am leaving tonight! If you will not sell it, I shall walk."

Pierre looked at him. Danny's eyes were no longer blue; they were a cold gray. "But what about Sawaquot?" Pierre spoke gently.

"The devil with Sawaquot!"

"He has saved your life twice, Daniel."

"And taken Jacques'." Danny's voice was bitter.

"No, my son. It was the others. He did what he thought he must do. Remember that the Indian has been mistreated by the English, even left to starve for lack of powder and ball. It would not have been so years ago when the red man used his bow and lived as his ancestors did; but now he depends on the white man and the white man's rum. He still believes that his French father will return, and has learned too late that the Treaty of Paris is signed and that all of the Northwest and Canada belong to the English."

"Treaty? What treaty, and when?" Danny was startled.

"The news came this spring, but it came too late. The tribes feel that they have been cheated and are more eager to fight than ever. It is only through Sawaquot that the Chippewa have not joined Pontiac."

Danny was silent. He had to admit that Pierre was right. What good could he do at Detroit? Why didn't Sir William Johnson send troops? Danny sat down heavily and stared into the fire. Any day now he expected to learn that he must go with the Chippewa back to Michilimackinac. The Chippewa would never allow him to remain at the fort—not with their constant fear of an attack.

Fork-in-the-Tree could not hold back the tribe forever. They would kill him as soon as they saw the first redcoat.

"You will not go, Danny?" Annette stood at his side.

Danny looked up and managed a wry smile. "Not to-night, Annette."

"But you must stay here always. . . ." Annette caught herself and turned away in confusion.

Danny only half heard her. He was looking into the flames. After a bit he took his musket from the corner and began to clean it. He was still there when Pierre came in to put out the lamp. The oil wick sputtered and died. Pierre stood looking at Danny in the firelight.

There was a sharp rap on the door. Pierre walked over and opened it. Fork-in-the-Tree strode into the room.

"Misquah, my brother, I must ask that you come to my lodge in the morning. A great canoe has been sighted heading this way, and it may be the Wyandottes return-ing. If so, you must stay with me for protection. I wish you might remain here, but my young men grow rest-less."

Filled with utter misery, Danny raised his head and looked at Sawaquot. He was a good man and a brave one. He had held the tribe together, risking his own life to save him. Danny knew that. All right, he would go, for now; but as soon as he could, he was heading for Detroit, regardless of what Pierre or the chief said.

Fork-in-the-Tree waited for an answer, watching Danny's face, reading his thoughts. Finally Danny spoke.

"I will be there, my father."

The Great Turtle Speaks

DANNY WENT back to the Indian lodge at dawn dressed in his greasy Indian garb again—but his red hair was long. He left before the others were awake, walking quickly away toward the fort.

Sawaquot and his family accepted him at their breakfast as though he had never gone away; and while they were eating, he learned about the canoe. It held not the returning Wyandottes, but a party of Iroquois from Fort Niagara. Danny could hardly finish his food in his excitement. Fort Niagara was where Sir William Johnson waited, trying to keep the tribes under control. Danny knew that it was from there that help must come, and he begged Sawaquot to take him to the council.

The chief agreed at last; and walking between White Elk and Fork-in-the-Tree, Danny joined the steadily mounting stream of Chippewa at the now empty house of the commandant.

They had no more than seated themselves when the Iroquois, tall, fine-looking warriors with fierce, beaked noses and towering scalp locks, walked silently into the hushed circle and seated themselves. Pipes were lighted and smoked. The leader of the Iroquois stood up and, raising a wampum belt, began to speak.

"Chippewa!" The Iroquois stood proudly, his voice

confident. "I have come with this belt to tell you that our great white father to the East, Sir William Johnson, is making ready for a great feast at Niagara. His fires are lighted and his kettles ready, and he asks you to attend with your friends of the Six Nations who have all made peace with the English. Our great white father says that if you do not come you shall all be destroyed, for the English are ready to march. Their war canoes are ready even now to move down upon you, and they will be joined by the mighty Iroquois and the other nations. Before the fall of the leaf, brothers, we will be back at Michilimackinac. What is your answer?"

An excited murmur arose among the Chippewa. Danny could hardly believe his ears. Help was on its way! The army was ready to march!

There was a hurried consultation among the chiefs. Sawaquot moved among them, talking and listening. Finally he turned and addressed the Iroquois.

"Our brothers the Iroquois have brought us welcome news. But before we give our answer we must consult the Great Turtle. As you know, it is our custom before undertaking a great journey to ask his advice. If the Great Turtle speaks and tells us to go, we will send twenty of our best braves to talk with the great white father. If not, we will remain in our lodges. I have spoken."

The chief sat down. A murmur like a crackling forest blaze swept the audience. The Iroquois left the council, gathering outside in a silent, scornful group.

When Sawaquot returned to his lodge, Danny was waiting.

"Tell me, Father," Danny said. "Who is the Great

Turtle, and why must we wait until he has spoken?"

"Quiet, Misquah!" White Elk came into the wigwam. "It is not for Englishmen that the Great Turtle speaks."

Sawaquot faced his son-in-law. "Let Misquah speak. He is our brother. Have you forgotten that long ago his white blood was washed away? And do not forget that when the English come with their fire sticks, Misquah will tell them of our friendship."

"I speak," White Elk said sullenly, "only to protect the secrets of our tribe."

"You spoke in haste, Wah-be-a-tik. Remember, it was Misquah who shared our lodge. It was Misquah who shot the mighty moose and the black bear."

White Elk drew himself up. His face was suddenly savage.

Danny, seated beside the chief, was puzzled. White Elk had been his friend. Now he was turning against him. Was it because he hated Englishmen, or was it because he was jealous of Danny's friendship with Sawaquot?

The brave was staring hard at Danny, hoping to make him drop his gaze. Slowly Danny rose to his feet.

"You are angry with me, my brother. Have I done you harm?" Danny's voice was low, but it held a hint of a threat. Taller and heavier than White Elk, Danny knew it would be an uneven contest if White Elk went for his knife. His own tomahawk, knife, and musket lay in back of him where he had left them upon entering the wigwam. Again Danny spoke. "Have I done you harm, Wah-be-a-tik?"

"Englishman, you and your king steal our lands. Even

now they have tricked the Iroquois into trying to frighten us. Are we old women?"

"Enough!" Sawaquot thundered. "We do not fight among ourselves."

White Elk seemed not to have heard. His hand moved toward the scalping knife at his belt. Danny's muscles tensed.

Suddenly the door of the lodge was thrown open. A voice said, "Misquah, Misquah, the hair has come off Annette's head." It was Little Sister.

White Elk's hand fell to his side. When he saw his daughter holding the doll up to Danny, his face softened.

"Forgive me, Misquah," he said.

"You are forgiven, Wah-be-a-tik."

"Sit at my side, my sons." It was Sawaquot who spoke. "There is pitch here to mend the doll of Little Sister. While you work, Misquah, I wish to speak to both of you."

Danny took the doll and resumed his seat beside the chief. White Elk sat next to him. The child stood beside Danny, watching him as he spread the pitch on the head of her "French doll."

Sawaquot's voice sounded weary. "Little Sister is wiser than we, my sons. To her there is no red or white. Only friends. This is as it should be among us." He turned toward Danny. "We are fierce and proud people, Misquah. In our anger we sometimes raise the hatchet against our own blood. It has always been so, but it saddens me." The chief's wrinkled face looked very old.

"I know, Father," Danny answered. "It is so among my people also."

The doll was finished. He held it out. White Elk rose to his feet.

"Take the doll to your mother, child," he said.

"Are you leaving, my son?" Sawaquot spoke kindly, as his granddaughter ran out of the wigwam.

"I go now," White Elk answered, "to speak to our young braves. Perhaps I can quiet them." He left the lodge.

Fork-in-the-Tree put his hand on Danny's arm. "I will tell you, Misquah, of our secret totem. You are the first Englishman ever to hear of this and the first who will see it. The Great Turtle is the totem of our tribe. We must await his answer before we can make reply to the great white father. You must know how my people tremble at the thought of going to Niagara. There will be many English soldiers at the fort. Their lodges will cover the ground and the big fire sticks on the walls can speak with thunder and with death. I have seen this place."

He pointed to a lodge pole from which hung his shields and weapons. "Do you see, Misquah, the medal that hangs there? Your chief, Sir William Johnson, gave it to me. I know the ways of the English, but even I tremble. Along with the soldiers will be the fierce Iroquois. My people fear a trap. Long ago we were at peace with the Iroquois but they turned upon us and drove us westward. Their canoes are swift and their lances many. The Englishman is their friend. Do you see our fear, Misquah?"

Danny nodded.

The chief continued. "And so we await the sign. To-night we build a lodge of logs and moosehide. If you wish, you may help us. I can tell you no more. Tonight the Great Turtle will speak!"

"And if he says that you are to go?"

"Then I will send deputies to Niagara."

Danny was silent, not daring to ask if he too might go to Niagara. Sawaquot said nothing. It was almost as if he were waiting for Danny to speak his thoughts. Finally, Danny could stand it no longer.

"My father," Danny said, "I wish to go with the deputies."

Fork-in-the-Tree nodded. "Does a father not know the heart of his son? It shall be my wish that you go to Niagara. Leave now; go to my sister's and make ready."

"I go." Danny took both of the chief's hands in his own. Then, snatching up his musket and ax, he ran out of the wigwam.

Pierre was waiting for him. He had seen Danny's tall figure bounding over the grass like a jack rabbit. His eyes lighted when he heard the news. Even Ahwun's dark face creased in a smile. Only Annette seemed unhappy. But Danny, hurriedly tying his new clothes into a bundle, was too excited to notice.

He left his pack with Pierre and raced back to the fort. He wanted to help build the lodge for the Great Turtle. As he reached the compound, he saw that logs were being cut and dragged to the fort. It took several hours to complete their task. Each log was of a different wood and each had to measure eight inches through and ten feet long. The poles were set into five holes, and some of the young men climbed up to the top to lash them together.

In the afternoon, moosehides were draped over them and tied fast with leather thongs. One side was left free for the medicine man to enter.

Again they took their axes and went after more wood and bark. As night fell, the wigwam was entirely covered with a round house of bark to shelter the council who would consult the Great Turtle.

Fires were lighted all around the skin tent. Danny, seated with Sawaquot and Wah-be-a-tik, thought that the whole village must have turned out for the event.

Then, straight through the door marched the gaudy figure of the medicine man. The tribe grew hushed. Two chiefs moved forward and lifted the sides of the tent so that the shaman could wriggle through. All was quiet.

Suddenly the huge cone began to shake. The sounds of many voices began to come from the inside. Some were yelling, some howling like wolves, some barking— all this mingled with screams and sobs and horrible mouthings. Danny shuddered. The sound was as if some- one were being put to a horrible death. Now and then an almost human voice cut through the unearthly din, but the sounds were unintelligible amidst the babblings.

Then silence. The tribe waited, breathless. All at once a low, feeble cry, like the mewings of a puppy, began. There was quick clapping of hands around the lodge.

"The Great Turtle!" they cried, over and over. The joy- ful clapping ceased, and they waited. This was the voice of the spirit who never lied.

Evil sounds began to come from the tent; and the taut, closely packed figures began to hiss loudly. A song started from the wigwam, then more voices, greeted by

clappings or hisses from the excited audience. A slight
pause and the voice of the medicine man was heard announcing the presence of the Great Turtle.

Sawaquot rose and put a large handful of tobacco into
the opening of the tent. He addressed the spirit. Were
the English going to make war on them and were there
many troops at Niagara?

The tent began to rock violently, and Danny's face
was wet with sweat as he stared in disbelief at the shaking skins. It wasn't possible for one man to shake the
huge structure in that way. It looked as though it were
ready to fall to the ground.

A great cry arose from inside the tent, and the shaman
was heard announcing the departure of the Great Turtle
for Niagara.

Minutes passed in absolute silence. The faces about
Danny were intent, watching, staring at the silent tent

lighted by the flickering fires. There came a weird gibbering, and again the wigwam shook. The chattering went on and on, then stopped. The medicine man spoke. The Great Turtle, he said, had gone as far as the fort, and there he had seen English soldiers as thick as leaves on the ground. They were making ready huge war canoes to attack those who did not join them.

Sawaquot stepped forward and again placed tobacco inside the flap. Would the Chippewa be received as friends if they went?

Again the weird gibberish, and again the medicine man translated. If the Chippewa went they would find Sir William Johnson eager to receive them. He would fill their canoes with presents of blankets and kettles and powder.

Instantly there were cries among those in the circle. "I will go, I will go." Sawaquot sat down, satisfied.

Now that these matters were settled, it was time for the people to ask questions. After what seemed like hours, Danny took his place at the side of the shaman's lodge. In his hand he held three sticks of tobacco that White Elk had given him. He thrust them under the flap of the tent. Instantly they were snatched from his hand.

"Tell me, oh Great Turtle." Danny's voice was hoarse. "What will happen to me?"

Again Danny heard the weird gibberish, followed by the voice of the medicine man. "You will return to Detroit, but when the leaves blow, you will return to Michilimackinac."

Danny wanted to ask more questions, but others were crowding around the tent.

He leaned close to Sawaquot and whispered, "I go, oh Father."

"It is well. Go to the cabin of Pierre and wait," the chief answered. "At dawn, come back. I shall see that you are given a place in a canoe. Sawaquot will keep his promise. You shall return to your people."

"Misquah thanks you, oh Chief," Danny said. "I shall return at dawn." He got to his feet and slipped silently past the excited Indians. He wanted to shout his excitement, to run and tell Pierre, but he forced himself to walk slowly until he was past the circle of squatting Chippewa, then he raced for the gates.

Outside the log palisade, Danny breathed easier. He had half expected to be challenged by a sentry but there had been no sign of one. Evidently all were at the moosehide wigwam.

He sped down the slope toward the beach. He could see a small light, dim in the window of Pierre's cabin. Danny reached the door and rapped sharply.

"Who knocks?" The voice was Pierre's, muffled by the heavy door.

"Danny. Let me in."

The door swung open. Pierre, in a long flannel nightgown, stood holding a candle and peering up at Danny. A red nightcap was pulled down to the top of his ears.

"Come in, come in," Pierre said.

"Pierre!" Danny cried, "I have great news."

"Good." Pierre held his fingers to his lips. "We must be quiet. The women sleep. Only Pierre wished to remain awake as it is better we two talk alone this night."

"How did you know I was leaving?" Danny asked.

"Does a hawk need to ask if the wind blows?" Pierre chuckled. "One look at your excited face and I knew the Great Turtle had spoken well. And do not look so disappointed. Old Pierre knows the Indian well. One had but to see the canoes of the Iroquois leaving to know that Sawaquot would send deputies."

"And I'm going with them." Danny, pacing up and down the small room, stopped suddenly in front of the fire. He faced his friend. "What will I find in Detroit, Pierre?"

The old man shrugged his shoulders. "Who knows?" Then seeing the look of concern on Danny's face, he added, "Try not to worry, boy. You have traveled a long journey since I first saw your frightened face in the store of Jacques Le Blanc. You are no longer a child. You must learn to think of today. Tomorrow will come, but if you are prepared. . . ."

"But Pierre. . . ."

"Sit down. You have not taken off your coat."

"I had forgotten." Danny shrugged out of his capote and dropped it on the floor. He sat down beside it, cross-legged, and stared into the fire. He was thinking of what the old man had said. Still, the thoughts of Detroit would not leave. Were his parents even now sitting in the kitchen thinking of him, or would he find a charred mound outside the walls? Or two mounds with two crosses?

"Tomorrow," Pierre spoke softly, "you will leave us perhaps forever. If now I speak of things which to you may sound foolish, forgive me. I forget that you are now a man. But then, I am old."

"And wise," Danny said.

"Perhaps," Pierre shrugged. "But do not be too sure. Wisdom does not always come with age. Sometimes it come to the young when they have lived many years in a short time. That is what you have done. And so when I speak of these things, it is not that I do not trust your wisdom. It is only that I wish you to reach home safely."

"Please go on, Pierre."

"First, do not trust the Chippewa. Sawaquot will not be with them. Tonight they think only of the gifts that Sir William will give them. Tomorrow they will fear his anger. Do not be surprised if only a few make the journey. And those that go will try many times to turn back. You must be ready. The Indian is a child. Never forget he can be a dangerous one."

"I couldn't," Danny said.

"When you reach Niagara," Pierre continued, "go to Sir William Johnson. Tell him you wish to join him in his march to Detroit.

"I think he will find a place for you. Perhaps in his army. If not, you will have to find another way. But again I warn you, stay close to the fort."

Danny turned his head and smiled. "You are so solemn, Pierre, not at all like the day I asked you to be my interpreter when I first came to Michilimackinac."

Pierre leaned forward and put his gnarled hand on Danny's sleeve. "I am solemn because we may never see you again," he said. "I am losing a son, Danny. But enough of that." He dropped his hand. "You will, if you are cautious and keep your temper, go down to Detroit at last. It will take you many days. I don't know how many.

An army travels slow, not like a brigade of north canoes but like a long heavy snake who has eaten too well.

"When you reach your home and if le bon Dieu is good, you will see your parents. And now I must speak of something else. Do not be surprised if it is not the same as when you left. That is all I have to say. Except this." Pierre knocked the ashes from his pipe and cleared his throat. "Jacques is dead. Only his goods and his store remain. But I will not forget him, nor will you. When the time comes, you will think of him, and perhaps of the north country. Think carefully then, my son, think of your home to the south, but do not forget your home to the north."

Danny got slowly to his feet. He looked down at Pierre. "And what is that time you speak of, Pierre? When will it come?"

Pierre shrugged. "Who knows?" he said. "Only now"—he stood up—"now it is time for bed. You leave at dawn. Did you speak to the Great Turtle?"

"Yes," Danny answered. "He said I would return to Michilimackinac."

"Will you?"

Danny looked at the floor. "I don't know, Pierre."

"It is not important now." Pierre managed a chuckle. He started for the sleeping room.

"Good night, Daniel, my son," the old man said.

Danny muttered something. It sounded like good-by.

The Snake

THE CANOES left a little after daybreak. There were only two of them. Pierre had been right. Out of the twenty men who had promised to go, only ten remained.

Danny, in the lead canoe, kept waving his hand at the small group of figures who stood a little to one side of the brightly blanketed Indians. After a while he could only see the blue-and-white-checked dress of Annette. Sawaquot, White Elk, Little Hawk, even Pierre had blended into the band of braves and squaws, children and dogs of the Chippewa.

Danny dipped his paddle hard. It hadn't been easy saying good-by, but now that it was over Danny felt a wild surge of excitement. He was going home.

They made their way across Lake Huron from island to island, finding most of the Indian villages empty and their inhabitants also on the way to Niagara. For four days the weather remained fair, until high winds forced them ashore at the carrying place at Taranto. They camped, then made a portage to the Lake aux Claires and set out again in a welter of gray waves. Soaked to the skin, they reached the other side; and while the others set about making a hut, Danny went for firewood.

The June woods were heavy with green leaves, and

blue jays screamed at him as he walked along. He found a pine stump that was well sheltered, and gathering an armful of splinters, Danny started back.

As he approached the others, a whirring sound made him stop and look about him. The whirring continued. He lowered his armful of wood to peer at the ground. Not two feet in front of him lay a thick snake. The blunt head was raised a little from the heavy coils and the rattles on the snake's tail buzzed like the shaking of a medicine man's rattle. Danny dropped the firewood and cocked his musket. The Chippewa saw him then, and Danny pointed excitedly toward the ugly reptile.

Before he could shoot, he found himself thrust aside. The Chippewa began to form a circle around the snake. Squatting down on their haunches, they filled their pipes, lighted them, and began to blow smoke at the coiled evil on the ground. Slowly the tightly coiled snake began to relax. He stopped his whirring warning as though he enjoyed the fragrant clouds of tobacco that drifted toward his blunt snout.

Puzzled, Danny lowered his musket and listened to the pleading of the Indians. "Oh grandfather," one said, "little grandfather, guide us on our journey and open the heart of Sir William Johnson to receive us. Give us many presents, oh grandfather, and protect our families in our absence."

Another begged the snake to forgive the Englishman who had tried to kill it and to stay among them rather than go back eastward among the English who were not friends of the great "Manito Kinibic" or snake-god.

The rattler, who had stretched himself contentedly on

the grass, seemed to grow weary of the speeches. Lowering his head, he started to slither away toward the west. Without thinking, Danny raised the butt of his gun and jerked it toward the rattler. In a flash the reptile turned and darted away to the east.

Danny walked toward the silent braves. They rose and knocked the ashes from their pipes to stand in an uncertain group, talking in low tones. Danny came up to them and waved his arm toward the canoes.

"Let us go on, my brothers. Our hut is but half finished, and we must hurry or we will arrive at Niagara too late."

"Misquah does not understand. The Manito has warned us to go back to our homes. We have decided to listen to him, and we are returning to our lodges." The braves stood watching Danny, their faces wooden and determined.

This was what Pierre had feared. Danny knew he must think fast, or they would never go to Niagara. You could never depend on Indians, he thought—the slightest excuse would serve them if they wished to change their minds.

"My brothers," Danny said, "the great Manito Kinibic has spoken to you and you have listened. But . . ." Suddenly Danny had an idea. He had frightened the snake into turning. It was his only chance, and he took it. "You have not listened closely enough. The Manito has come to lead us to Sir William. Did he not disobey your request and go eastward? Are you old women, that you fear to follow?"

They stood grunting among themselves like a bunch of red sows. Finally they seemed to agree. Putting their pipes in their pouches, they straggled back toward the unfinished hut. Danny saw them begin covering the framework with bark. Their faces were sullen, but he knew that he had won. Calling them old women was too much for the pride of the Chippewa. Danny, muttering a word of thanks to the snake for moving away from his musket, tried not to think what would have happened if his companions had grown angry or if the rattlesnake had gone westward.

The next morning the canoes were dragged ashore and hidden under a pile of branches. Then, taking up their packs, they set off along a narrow trail toward Lake Ontario.

Now Danny's pack strap cut into his forehead like an iron hoop. Mosquitoes rose in gray clouds to light on his hands and face, their stings piercing him like fiery porcupine quills. He wished he had covered himself with bear grease like the others. Brushing the insects away from his mouth, he trudged along, slapping and fighting the maddening swarm, crushing the buzzing bodies that were heavy with his blood.

That night they built a huge smudge and slept in the smoke.

Noon of the next day saw them making new canoes on the shores of Lake Ontario. They worked for two days, stripping bark from birches into sheets eighteen feet long, then sewing the ends with "wattape." By nightfall of the third day they had put in ribs and bars and the canoes were finished. The next evening found them camped four miles from Fort Niagara.

Danny urged them to go on to the fort, but they refused to listen. They would approach the fort in the morning, they said, or not at all. Several times Danny feared they would turn back. He spent most of the night trying to reassure them that they were not walking into a trap. At last he slept, worn out from ceaseless questions and childish fears.

When dawn came, Danny awoke to see the Chippewa squatting along the riverbank, painting their faces with the brightest colors they could find. Then they rose and, singing a song they used when going into danger, they loaded the canoes and headed for Point Missisaki, which lay directly across from the fort. As soon as they reached the point, Danny, after bathing in the river and changing into his new clothes, helped them to unload. Then he took one of the canoes and paddled for the fort.

Never had Danny seen such a gathering. Everywhere he looked he saw the gaudily painted figures of Indians from every nation striding about the fort under the muzzles of English cannon glowering down from the walls. There were Menomini from Green Bay, Ottawa from Detroit, Mississauga whose villages they had passed on their trip east, Caughnawaga from Canada, Wyandottes whom Danny scanned carefully, hoping for a glimpse of Joe Loup, and a great host of Iroquois.

The neat tents of the soldiers stood in rows against the gray stone bastions of the fort, while the soldiers, in brilliant scarlet coats over shining white breeches, wandered in and out of the tents, or drilled in glittering squares to the shouted orders of their drill masters. The English words sent a thrill of pleasure through Danny, but he couldn't bring himself to approach any of the soldiers. He chose instead a group of French Canadians who were looking on and laughing among themselves. This was the group that looked the best to him. "Pardon, mes amis." Danny addressed what appeared to be the leader of the group. "I am looking for the tent of Sir William Johnson."

"Ah, so?" the small voyageur grinned. "And so does everyone in this place. The English offer presents, and pouf—every Indian and Frenchman within a hundred mile come to get his share. Where are you from, M'sieu?"

"Michilimackinac," Danny answered.

Another voyageur spoke up. "You perhaps knew the great Jacques Le Blanc."

"I was his commis," Danny answered.

"So? You perhaps can tell us of his death. We have heard that he died at the hands of the Chippewa."

"It is true," Danny answered. "But I have no wish to speak of it. Now I seek Sir William."

"To get your fifty sous a day?"

"For what?" Danny asked.

"For marching to Detroit. Name of a cabbage, but he should give you one hundred. You are big enough." The voyageurs laughed heartily.

"Perhaps I will join," Danny said. "Now, please, M'sieu, where is the tent of Sir William Johnson?"

"It is useless. He does not care to see Canadian. Besides, he is not in a tent, but in the fort. See the large building that looks like a château where the sentry argues with that group of Indians? Name of a pipe, look at the Indians. We had better stay together, friends. There may be hair lifted tonight."

Danny followed the voyageur's pointing finger. Then he was running off across the parade ground. The Indians around the sentry were his Chippewa!

"What is your hurry, M'sieu?" Danny didn't answer. The Canadian shrugged. "It seems," he said to the others, "that I have heard stories of that red-haired one."

Danny reached the door leading into Sir William's quarters. His Chippewa stood in a small circle about a single sentry. Their faces were sullen. Danny could see that they had been sampling trade rum.

There was a sudden scuffle. The sentry, young and frightened, raised the butt of his musket. With one stride, Danny was in the center of the Chippewa. He was just in time. Strong Wolf, with a snarl, had snatched his tomahawk from his belt and was waving it in the sentry's face. Danny's hand closed over the wrist of the angry brave. With a quick twist, he pinned Strong Wolf's arm in back of him and forced him against the wall.

"Mah-hen-gun is hasty!" Danny's eyes flashed dangerously. "The Chippewa act like old women. They are mah-na-dud, bad, bad."

The brave grunted angrily.

Danny released him and quickly turned to the others. "What would your chief say if he saw you now? Go back to your lodges, white coyotes, before the white father sends soldiers to burn your wigwams."

The Chippewa shrank back as though they had been struck. To be called coyotes and old women—Misquah was mad!

"Go," Danny said. He pointed toward the river. "Go

home without presents. Tell Sawaquot that Misquah sent you!"

Ten pairs of eyes glared at him. There was murder there. Danny stood his ground. At his back the sentry, his musket raised fearfully, looked on in amazement. At any moment he expected one of the braves to strike this tall voyageur dead. Nothing happened. Slowly the Chippewa relaxed, and their hands dropped from their weapons. It was Strong Wolf who spoke.

"Misquah, do not send us back without presents. This Englishman would not let us in."

Danny half turned to the young sentry but he kept his eyes still on the Chippewa. "Is this true? Did you refuse to let them enter?" he asked.

The sentry only stared. Danny realized that he had spoken in Chippewa.

"Don't be frightened," Danny said in English. The half-forgotten words sounded strange to him. He couldn't help but smile.

The boy seemed to gain sudden courage from this amazing voyageur who spoke English.

"They can go in now, sir," he said, "but it looked like trouble before you came."

"I will take them to Sir William," Danny answered. He raised his hand. "Come," he said in Chippewa.

The ten Indians followed him as meekly as if they had been sheep.

The sentry grounded his musket and wiped his forehead with the back of his sleeve. He wondered who the red-haired man was.

Danny entered a dark hall. To his left was an open

door guarded by two more scarlet-coated sentries. He walked forward, the Chippewa at his heels. The sentries brought up their muskets to bar his way.

"Who goes?"

"Daniel O'Hara, of Michilimackinac and Detroit." Danny spoke in English.

"You don't look English," one sentry said.

Danny stared down at the soldiers. "I am here to see Sir William. Is there any reason why I shouldn't?"

"Let him pass!"

Danny looked at the speaker. He was seated at the head of a long table. His uniform was heavy with gold braid and across his shoulders was a scarlet blanket. Face florid, eyes frosty, he stared at Danny for a moment, then said something to the officer at his side.

The sentries lowered their muskets. Danny stepped forward. This was Sir William Johnson, he decided. Who else would wear the ceremonial blanket of a Mohawk chief? He reached the table and stood waiting for Sir William to speak. On either side of him, standing proudly, were twelve Mohawks. Black eyes glittering, scarlet blankets hanging from their wide shoulders, they stared contemptuously at the Chippewa.

Danny heard a mutter at his side. Strong Wolf was gazing with envy at the gold braid on the border of the Mohawk blankets.

Danny grounded his musket, folding his hands across the muzzle.

"Your name?"

"Daniel O'Hara."

Sir William leaned back in his carved chair and waved

a white hand. "Why are you here, O'Hara, an Englishman?"

"I have come from Michilimackinac, Sir William," Danny said.

"You know my name? That is more than I expected from a voyageur." He gave Danny a frosty smile. "So you are from Michilimackinac?"

"Yes, sir," Danny said. "And Detroit."

The officers exchanged glances.

"I thought there were no English at Michilimackinac. Are you a renegade?" The baronet's eyes were cold.

"I was a prisoner of the Chippewa," Danny said. His eyes were equally cold.

Sir William leaned forward. "Do you mean that you were caught in the massacre?"

"I was. For the last year I have lived with Chief Sawaquot."

"Amazing!" Sir William leaned back in his chair. "Forgive me for calling you a renegade.

"Major, take these Chippewa with O'Hara and give them presents. I imagine that is what they are here for. I will talk with them later. My Mohawks will go with you. Right now, I want to hear more about this matter.

"Sit down, O'Hara." Sir William pointed to the chair where the major had been sitting.

Danny sat down, his musket across his knees, and wondered how to begin.

"Perhaps you should start with the day you left your home for high adventure." Sir William's eyes twinkled.

"Yes, sir." It all seemed too long ago to Danny, but as

he began his story he forgot the room and Sir William in the telling of his two years.

When he had finished, Sir William spoke. "I can readily see why you are anxious to return to Detroit. I suppose you would like to join my army?"

"That I would, Sir William," Danny said.

"We shall see. When you first came into the room I very nearly gave you a command right there. Did you know that?"

"No, sir."

"But now, I am not so sure that the army is the place for you. First, let me ask another question. What will you do when you reach Detroit?"

Danny shook his head. "If my parents are alive I'll stay, I guess. I had hoped to start a trading post with my father, but now I haven't a thing left to show for my two years' work."

"Haven't you? What about your experience? The army has need of scouts; the country will need young men like you. This year has been a year of disaster. Perhaps you did not know about Fort Pitt, Fort Le Boeuf, Fort Venango, Detroit, all of them surrounded by Indians. Settlers massacred, tortured, captured. Not only the settlements of Virginia, but Pennsylvania as well. Amherst has called the Indian uprising only temporary. You see the results of his foolishness. But enough of past mistakes. We are ready to renew the war, and perhaps with better results."

"What are you planning to do, sir?" asked Danny.

Johnson didn't appear to have heard. He rose to his feet and strode up and down the room. "It needn't have happened—any of it. Before we took Canada, all of the tribes, jealous of the French, looked to us to protect them. Instead the Indian received nothing but brutality at our hands. Even the Iroquois, long our friends, have been tempted to revolt. And now we have this problem which is of our own doing. The Indian is brave and loves his freedom. Even if we wished to, we could not exterminate him. There is only one way to end the struggle, and that is to start treating him with respect and attention. In order to keep friction of white settlements from angering him, we should buy land farther west for our use."

"But what will happen when more and more settlers come west?" asked Danny.

"Ah. I see that I have not misjudged you, O'Hara." Sir William allowed himself a frosty smile. "That will be another problem. The Indian will be forced farther west to his eventual doom." He spread his hands. "But what else is to be done? We cannot tame him; we cannot give up the land."

"It is a good land," Danny said. "It's hard, but it's good."

"You have learned that, eh? I thought so. And now I suppose you wonder why I have told you all of this."

"I do wonder. I never knew these things. My father once spoke of you and of Amherst." Danny stopped there. He had spoken as though his father were already dead. But he forced himself to go on. "When I left for Niagara, I thought, now there will be peace. My mother, sir, often spoke of peace. I have never really known what it was."

"My mother also spoke thus," said Sir William. "Now it seems that I have forgotten the meaning of the word. You may live to see it, boy. I never will. But it is worth fighting for, O'Hara, and you can help."

"Me, sir?" Danny looked at Sir William in amazement. "What can I do? I can never forget what the Indians did."

Sir William said nothing for a moment. When he finally spoke, his voice was soft. "I too have lost friends, O'Hara, and at the hands of the Indians. And yet the Indians are my friends, many of them. Perhaps if we were to forget that we are red man and white, but rather all men, we would feel differently. There are evil men on all sides, O'Hara. As I remember, this killer of your friend Jacques was himself a Canadian."

Danny scowled till the scar on his forehead burned red. "I still hope to find Joe Loup."

"Your chance may come. But after that, what? I tell you, my son, the future of the colonies will depend on men like yourself. Men raised in this country, men who understand the Indian and can deal with him."

"But how?" Danny stared at the floor. "I left home hoping to come back a rich young trader. Look at me now. I'm no better than a squaw man. I've lived with the Indians so long that I've forgotten how to act among civilized people."

"A failure at sixteen, eh?"

Danny didn't answer.

"All right, O'Hara, I'll give you a chance. You go home. On the way you keep an eye on Bradstreet and our pitiful army. See how he governs it. Then when you arrive

at Detroit, if you arrive, you think about what I have said. If you decide not to continue as a trader, you come back to Niagara and I will see that you are given a commission as scout. But before you decide, I want you to think of your friend Jacques. What would he have done? Would he sit here as you are now, complaining about his failure, or would he start all over?"

"You don't understand. . . ."

"Good day to you, sir. You may join the Canadians on our march to Detroit."

Danny, in his camp that night, thought of Sir William's strange speech. What did it all mean? Did this powerful man who was bringing about peace with the tribes want him to join the army or become a trader? Well, Danny thought, he would have plenty of time to decide. First he had to reach Detroit.

Detroit

THE FOUR weeks that followed were much worse than even Sir William Johnson had foretold. Danny, traveling with the Canadians, found himself at a loss to understand how a man like Colonel Bradstreet, who had led three thousand men to capture Fort Frontenac during the French War, could make so many mistakes. His soldiers, the glittering army that Danny had expected, turned out to be sickly and ill-disciplined. It was a poor excuse for an army that marched on July 10 for Fort Schlausser above the great falls of Niagara.

Twenty days after leaving Schlausser, they landed at Sandusky. Bradstreet, who had been ordered to attack and destroy the Wyandottes, Miamis, and Ottawa camped there, parlayed instead. That night there was feasting in the Indian camps. They had tricked the English again.

By now Danny had become used to the seething discontent around him. He was beginning to understand what Sir William had told him about the army, and any thoughts of becoming a scout were gone. All that he cared for now was the river ahead, and he prayed that they would reach Detroit in time.

Finally, on the twenty-sixth of August, they saw the approaching lodges of the Wyandottes. Instantly the air was filled with war whoops. Muskets cracked as the Wyandottes rushed down to the water's edge to greet the boats in a false show of welcome. But Danny took little notice—he was straining his eyes to catch the first glimpse of Fort Detroit.

From the distant spot of brown that marked the log stockade came a flash of light followed by a dull boom. A faint puff of blue smoke drifted up into the air. Cannon smoke, but to Danny it looked like a flying pennant of welcome. Danny began to gather his gear together. Each stroke of the sweeps brought the barges closer to the fort. He could make out the walls now more clearly; and there, still flying, the tattered Cross of Saint George! Danny let out a whoop—he was coming home!

The barges swung in toward shore. Cheer after cheer surged out of the bullet-scarred fort. The ramparts were black with wildly shouting settlers. Danny rubbed his eyes. A mist seemed to be blurring the outlines of those around him.

Drums rattled like musketry across the torn earth. Danny scrambled out of the barge and started for the fort. He looked about him in a pounding surge of excitement.

Row after row of red-coated troops passed him and disappeared between the open gates, swallowed up by the cheering defenders. The Highlanders, in their green and black tartans of the Black Watch, were swinging along to the fierce skirl of the pipers, while just behind them walked the haughty and fearless Iroquois watching the rows of yelling Wyandottes with savage contempt.

Danny and the Canadians were the last to enter the gate. Instantly the ranks broke as the settlers poured among them, laughing, crying, cheering—their haggard faces wild with joy. Danny forced his way through the crowd, searching for his mother and father.

The gateway was so solidly packed with troops and settlers that Danny felt himself being pulled along with the crowd. Here and there a familiar face flashed in the surging welter of bodies around him, only to be caught up and whirled on. Thin arms wrapped in tattered uniforms waved muskets and cheered the relieving garrison. Bradstreet, his face red and perspiring, strutted like a rooster up and down in front of his troops. A long line of prisoners stood glowering sullenly at the crowd. They were a ragamuffin lot of half-breeds and Indians who had joined Pontiac and now awaited their fate. Danny scanned their faces briefly.

There was Major Gladwyn, thin and haggard, talking to the colonel. Danny hardly recognized him for the trim officer that he had been. Gladwyn and Bradstreet, flanked by their staffs, seemed to have reached some sort of decision. The drums began again, and the soldiers formed a square about the prisoners.

Suddenly Danny forced his way through the mob, running. He had seen a small, bandy-legged figure, with a bristly shock of white hair, arguing violently with a red-coated provincial. A small knot of Wyandottes barred Danny's way. Using his musket, Danny started through. There was a muttered curse. Danny whirled in his tracks. He saw a painted face snarling French oaths, the face of Joe Loup!

Danny was after him in a flash

Danny was after him in a flash. The Canadian ducked out of the thinning crowd and sped for the gates. Danny shouted and tried to level his musket, but by the time he had freed himself from the crowd, Joe Loup had disappeared around the corner of the gate. Danny bent low in pursuit. A Wyandotte stepped in front of him! Danny knocked the Indian to the ground. He cleared the prostrate body with a long leap and, reaching the gate, paused to look quickly about him. He saw Joe then, running toward a canoe. Danny raised his gun. Crack! The musket jerked in his hands. He saw the fleeing figure stumble, then right itself and turn toward the woods. Danny flung his heavy gun to the ground and raced after him.

He pounded down the hard-beaten path, then cut across the grass. Joe had reached the open meadow. He was getting away! Frantically, Danny twisted and turned in among the stumps. Joe was already halfway to the woods when he began to stagger. Danny felt a stab of hope—he had hit Joe with his first shot. Now the fleeing man appeared to stumble again. This time he fell flat on the ground!

With a glad shout, Danny raced toward him. There was a loud report, and a ball whizzed close to Danny's ear. Danny ducked, then doubled his speed. He was gaining fast, and Joe wouldn't have time to reload. He saw him spring to his feet and stumble into the woods. Joe Loup was heading straight for the cabin of Jacques Le Blanc!

Danny leaped a ditch and sped on after the fleeing murderer, trying desperately to think what Jacques had once said about an extra canoe. He couldn't remember, but he knew he must beat Joe to the cabin.

The woods were ahead of him then, and Danny called himself a fool for throwing away his musket. He jerked his tomahawk free and plunged into the underbrush to halt, listening. Joe might be waiting in ambush. There was a sudden crackling of limbs ahead. Danny bent low to the ground and fairly flew through the trees. He burst into the clearing, his breath a raw rasp in his chest, and stopped.

His eyes swept the tangled opening. Jacques' cabin stood just as he had left it, but Danny saw something else! Joe Loup, the Wolf, the murderer, was getting away. He stood in the stern of a birchbark canoe, paddling with all his might toward the bend in the river that would hide him from Danny's sight forever.

Joe saw Danny then. He laughed wildly, cursing him. Danny half ran, half fell down the bank into the shallows. He drew back his arm. With all his might he sent the tomahawk whirling toward the escaping Joe Loup. The blade flashed in the sunlight, then splashed harmlessly into the river, half a canoe's length from the grinning figure in the stern.

Danny slumped down in the mud, letting the water seep into his leggings. Joe Loup had escaped.

Suddenly Danny stared at the bobbing craft. Something was wrong! Joe Loup wasn't laughing now—he was trying frantically to turn the canoe toward the opposite bank. Danny caught a glimpse of the man's face—it was a mask of terror. The canoe was wallowing like a wounded animal.

All at once the bow shot up into the air. As the canoe plunged down and sank out of sight, Joe screamed once—the wild terrible cry of a drowning man—then silence. The waters of the river flowed on, black and cold. Something moved on the surface and bobbed downstream. It was a single hawk's feather.

Danny lay back on the riverbank, weak with exhaustion. He remembered now what Jacques had said. He had left one canoe because it had a hole in the side—and Joe Loup couldn't swim a stroke. Jacques had won after all. Joe Loup was dead!

After a while, Danny stood up and started back for the fort.

The Decision

DANNY SLOWED only long enough to retrieve his musket from the grass outside the fort, then he was inside the gates again, hoping for the sight of his father. From the crowded square in front of the bullet-scarred houses came the smell of roasting meat. Someone had taken a steer from a Canadian farmer, and they were preparing a barbecue.

Danny forced his way through the crowd, hoping for a familiar face. A woman in a patched sunbonnet, her thin face pinched, eyes dark with grief, stood leaning against a scarred signpost. Danny, glancing up, saw the well-remembered sign of Meeker's trading post. It was only then that he realized the woman was Mrs. Meeker.

Danny started toward her. She was the first white woman he had seen in two years. In spite of her haggard appearance, Danny felt an almost uncontrollable urge to hear her speak.

"Mrs. Meeker," he said. Danny pulled off his hat.

The woman stared at him with lackluster eyes.

"Don't you know me?" he asked. "I'm Danny O'Hara."

"Danny O'Hara is dead. Mr. Meeker is dead." She turned away.

Danny took her gently by the arm. The arm seemed almost fleshless.

"Look, Mrs. Meeker," he pleaded. "I'm Danny O'Hara. Where is my mother?"

The woman tried to pull away from him. Deep in her shadowed eyes something flared and went out. She began to whimper.

"Leave the woman alone now, or I'll be callin' the guard." A rough hand seized Danny's arm. Danny let go of the frightened woman and whirled around. Red-faced, bristled chin thrust forward, Michael O'Hara glared up at him.

"The O'Hara!" Danny shouted. Cat-quick, he seized his father by the front of his coat and lifted him off the ground.

"Put me down, ye spalpeen, or I'll knock the stuffin's out of ye!" The O'Hara struggled to free himself, but Danny, laughing, held him easily.

"Don't you know me, O'Hara?"

"Know ye?" His father was nearly exploding with wrath. Suddenly his eyes flew wide and his bristled chin dropped. "Danny," he said. The pink face crumpled. "Danny, me boy!"

Danny released his father. The little man's arms went around him.

"I've come home, Pa."

"So ye have, my son." The O'Hara stepped back, wiping his eyes. "Faith, but ye've growed. Wait till your mother sees ye."

"Where is she, Pa? Is she well?"

"Fine as frog's hair, boy. Come along, let's not be standin' here. Your mother's in the store."

Danny was up the store steps in a single bound.

"Mary, Mary!" Close at his heels came the O'Hara, waving his arms and shouting.

"What is it, O'Hara?" She saw Danny then and for a moment it looked as though she would fall. "Danny," she wailed. "You're home . . ." Her arms went around her son.

The O'Hara's voice was tender. "Sure and she's been that worried. We've missed you, boy."

"I know," said Danny. "I know."

"We thought you were dead." Mary O'Hara looked up into his face. Her hand shook as she gently pushed Danny's red hair from his forehead.

Danny smiled down at her. "The luck of the Irish," he said and smiled.

Mary O'Hara began to cry.

"Faith now, Mother, don't take on so." The O'Hara dabbed at his eyes. "The boy is home and well from the looks of him. And here comes Mrs. Meeker. Danny nearly scared the wits out of her."

"Sit down, Danny." His mother smiled through her tears. "I'll see to the poor thing and then we can talk. Come along, Mrs. Meeker; sure and it's time you were takin' your nap." She led the gaunt woman into the back room.

Later, when the shouts of the revelers outside had quieted, candles still burned inside the store. There had been an endless stream of visitors. Everyone in the fort, it seemed, had heard of Danny's homecoming and had stopped to shake his hand. Danny failed to recognize most of the visitors, but his father, face glowing with pride, greeted each one by name. His bandy legs carried him first to the door, back to Danny, and then to the door again as each new visitor arrived and left.

"My son," he would say, "survived the massacre, he did. Sure and he's growed." The scarecrow inhabitants of the fort would shake hands, then O'Hara would shoo them out. Finally, puffing with excitement, he barred the door.

Mary O'Hara, smiling now, sat next to her son. Her thin fingers were clasped over Danny's hand.

"Now would you believe it, Mother?" Michael said. "Would you believe it was the same folks as was here a year ago? Comin' in, they were, just to shake me hand. Things have changed, Danny, my boy."

"They have, Pa."

The O'Hara hitched a chair close to his son. "Now, will you be tellin' us of travels, lad—and where," he winked at Danny, "have you put all your furs?"

"There aren't any furs, Pa."

"No furs?" The O'Hara rocked back in his chair. "But I thought. . . ."

"Shame on you, Michael O'Hara," Mary said. "Can't you be forgettin' that for now?"

"I'm sorry, Pa," Danny said.

"Don't you be botherin' about it," the O'Hara said, but Danny could see the disappointment in his father's face.

"Tell us about yourself, son," Mary O'Hara said.

"There's a lot to tell, Mother. But first, how does it happen you're living here instead of at the farm?"

"The farm was burnt," his mother answered sadly.

"And good riddance," the O'Hara snorted.

"How can you say that, Michael?" Mary sounded hurt.

"I can say it easy, Mother. Danny remembers how I hated that farm. Grubbin' mornin' and night around stumps as big as a horse."

"Sure, I remember," Danny smiled. Somehow his parents' bickering didn't seem to bother him tonight. It was familiar. There was even something warm about it.

"Mr. Meeker was killed," Mary said. "His poor wife was near crazy with the grief."

"And your mother nursing her like a child," the O'Hara finished.

"And you acting like you owned the place," she said.

"Now, Mother," the O'Hara sputtered.

"It's just the same," Danny said. "I guess I wouldn't know I was home if you and Pa weren't fighting a little."

Mary O'Hara smiled. "We do go around a bit, Danny. But your father is a fine man and a brave one."

The O'Hara stopped his rocking. "Now would you listen to that! The first time in years that your mother has admitted my sterling worth."

"Go along with you, Michael."

"Faith and it's true, Danny. Never a finer woman lived than your mother there. We've had our differences, but usually it was me as was causin' them."

"Now Michael, it ain't so," Mary said.

"I think it was the farm," Danny said.

"I wouldn't say that, boy. Your mother was right in a way. It was the farm and the hog that saved our lives and some of the fort too."

"The hog?" Danny said. "I was hoping you'd have that when I came home. Seems like I've thought of nothing but food for the past four weeks."

"Saints preserve us." Mary got to her feet. "Here Danny comes home hungry and we haven't fed him a bite. Put the kettle on, O'Hara, whilst I get some of that corn-meal mush."

"Corn-meal mush," Danny grinned. "Think I should go after bear?"

"And run away again?" His father began to chuckle in short gasps.

"That's nothing to be laughin' about, O'Hara," Mary said. She moved the iron pot closer to the flames.

"It's all over now, Mother." Danny got up and stood beside her. "Maybe it was all for the best." Then he sobered. "You knew that Jacques was dead?"

"Dead? How?" The O'Hara stood at his elbow. "Here we've been gabbin' instead of hearin' about your adventures."

"He can tell us after he's eaten, Michael." Mary began stirring the pot. "Get a dish for the boy, and I'll serve us some mush."

To Danny's surprise, the mush tasted delicious. There was even a little sugar to go with it. When he had eaten his fill, he began his story.

The room was quiet except for the crackling of the fire. Outside, an occasional burst of song or the sound of passing voices told that the fort was still celebrating the end of the siege. When Danny finished his story, his voice was hoarse. His mother hadn't spoken a word during the whole time of the telling. Even the O'Hara had limited his interruptions to grunts and occasional mild cussing which Mary silenced with a glance.

"And now tell me about Detroit," Danny said.

"We're alive, saints be praised, but no thanks to Pontiac." Mary sighed. "Sure and it's like heaven havin' the boy back, isn't it, O'Hara?"

"That it is, Mary. Now let's be forgettin' the siege for a bit and let Danny talk."

But Mary was watching her son's face. "Let him rest, Michael. The poor lad is tired out."

"No," said Danny. He sat up straight. "I want to hear about the siege. It's been two long years since I've heard any news."

"Two years." The O'Hara shook his head. "The years were long here too. Two years of starvin', fightin', and dyin'. Seein' the town gaunt with famine. Learnin' of the fall of Michilimackinac, Venango, Pitt, and the others. We thought you were dead. It was hard here."

"The land is hard on the frontier," Danny said. A slow drowsiness was creeping over him. He had to force himself awake. "Sir William Johnson told me . . ." His voice trailed off.

"You saw Sir William?" The O'Hara snorted. "What did the old turkey gobbler have to say?"

"He offered me a commission as scout," Danny mumbled.

"A scout! Faith, Mary. Did you hear that? A scout with Johnson."

"Hush." Mary's voice was tender. "The lad is asleep. He looks as though he'd never been away except for that deep scar on his poor head."

" 'Tis a deep scar," the O'Hara said. "And how we'll ever be gettin' this young giant to bed is more than I know."

"I'll be makin' a pallet on the floor for him."

"Faith, 'twill be softer than a barge."

Danny awoke at daybreak. His first move was to reach for his musket. Instead his hand touched the rough floor. He sat up, puzzled.

"Danny, lad." His mother's voice came from the room at the rear. "Is that you awake?"

"It is, Mother." Danny stretched and got to his feet. The front door swung wide and in came the O'Hara.

"Mornin' to you, son," the O'Hara beamed. "Are you feelin' fit, boy?"

"Fine as frog's hair." Danny grinned.

"Good. Then we can be talkin' business before your mother comes in. Now sit down and tell me about them furs of yours."

"I don't want to talk about them now, Pa."

"And why not? Are you grown so big that you don't wish to tell your father anythin'? Why are ye so mum? Not bringin' those furs that Jacques promised sort of changes things. Is it that you've decided to go with Johnson?"

"No," Danny said stubbornly, "I don't want to go with Johnson. I don't know what I want to do. I had planned to come home and help you by starting a store. I ran away so that I could come home rich. Well, I'm home but I'm poor. It seems so hopeless, almost as though we were back where we were two years ago."

"What is it, son?" Mary came into the room. "Sure

and let's be havin' a bite of breakfast before we talk. Look, I'll be gettin' the silver mugs for cider."

Danny and his father sat down at the table, the O'Hara scowling, Danny staring moodily at the toe of his moccasin.

Mary O'Hara crossed to the cupboard and took down two silver mugs. She was just about to pour the cider when she stopped, a look of amazement on her face. A piece of folded paper lay in the bottom of the tankard.

Danny saw her coming toward him. She was holding the paper as though it burned her fingers.

"It's the strangest thing, Danny. Sure and I'm wonderin' if the little folk have been here. The letter was folded nice and neat in the silver mug and it has your name on it."

"Let me see it."

Danny unfolded the paper. His lips moved silently as he began reading. All at once Danny let the paper fall to the table.

"Have you seen a ghost, boy?" The O'Hara rose to his feet.

Danny found his voice. "The letter is from Jacques," he said in a whisper.

"From Jacques?" Mary crossed herself.

The O'Hara snapped his fingers. "I remember. When Jacques came to see us, he asked for a bit of paper and ink. He must have left it in the tankard for you, Danny."

"I guess I'd better read it to you," Danny said. "It's in French, so I'll have to go slow. It starts out, 'Red Head.' That's what Jacques called me."

"Go on, boy," the O'Hara said.

Danny swallowed hard. He continued. "This is to tell you that in case I do not return to Detroit, if something should happen to me, all my furs, my goods, and my storehouse shall go to you, Daniel O'Hara." There was more, and Jacques' signature, but Danny didn't want to read it aloud. His parents were watching him anxiously.

"I now own over eight thousand dollars' worth of furs, eight canoes, a storehouse . . ." Danny seemed stunned.

His father was pounding him on the shoulders. "You're a rich man, boy. Just think, Mary. With me and Danny workin' this store, we can have one of the best posts in the territory. O'Hara and Son."

"And you'll be stayin' here, Danny?" his mother asked.

Danny got to his feet and his eyes had a faraway look. "Jacques has left me all of this for a reason, and now I think I have my answer. The Great Turtle said I would return to Michilimackinac, and I must. I hope that you understand. . . ."

"But we need you, Danny," his mother said.

Danny took her hand. "No," he said. "I think you will do better by yourselves. I could never be happy working in the store. But I will see to it that you and Pa have everything you need. The O'Hara is a good storekeeper, and you'll never need to be hungry or afraid any more. I have to go back. I want to help build this new land. I've seen massacres and yet I've lived with the Indians. I can speak French, English, and Chippewa. I can paddle a canoe, hunt, trade. I'm no longer a boy running away because he lost his father's musket. I'm a man of the North, as the voyageurs say. It was the fur trader who opened the frontier; it will be the fur trader who will push it westward, and I want to be with them. That is what Jacques would have wanted."

The O'Hara shook his head. "I don't understand you, lad."

Mary O'Hara smiled sadly. "You should, Michael. Have you forgotten why we left Philadelphia?"

The O'Hara began to chuckle. "Faith, and when you put it that way, Mary. . . ." His arm went around his wife's shoulders. "I guess the boy should have his chance. After all, he is O'Hara's son!"

Danny smiled. "I think, Pa, that maybe we had better hunt some squirrel for breakfast. All right, Mother?"

"I think squirrel would taste very good." Mary O'Hara pulled her son's head down and kissed him quickly on the cheek.

Danny picked up his musket, powder horn, and shot pouch. Slipping the straps over his shoulder, he opened the door. "Coming, Pa?"

"Sure, I'll be right with you."

Then Danny was down the steps, striding away toward the river.

World Reborn

The Young Voyageur started out to be a story about Mackinac Island, its commanding fort and harbor. It wasn't until actual research began that the powerful story of the older Fort Michilimackinac began to unfold. And so I changed the setting and the time to include one of the most exciting events in Michigan's history—Pontiac's War.

An early edition of *The Travels and Adventures of Alexander Henry,* recently republished as *Attack at Michilimackinac,* gave me an eye-witness account of the events of those colorful years. But what about the fort itself? What did it actually look like to Danny O'Hara? Old maps only identified buildings. How was it built? A reconstructed palisade fallen into disrepair and the view of the Straits of Mackinac were all that remained in 1954. With only these to work with I wrote and illustrated this book. It was published in 1955.

And then, four years later, wonder of wonders, work began, based on sound archaeological and historical evidence, to reconstruct this fort of my dreams. From 1959 to 1962 I followed every detail and in that year wrote and illustrated *The Big Dig* telling of the important work in progress. Every year since then has seen the excavation of additional areas of the fort and the reconstruction of the discovered buildings.

Today, Fort Michilimackinac stands as a living marker of the world of Danny O'Hara, Jacques, Annette, Sawaquot, and all of the characters in these pages. To walk beneath the Land Gate into this 18th Century world reborn, is always a thrill. And as each new building rises, the thrill grows.

For those of you who have enjoyed reading *The Young Voyageur,* I can only hope that you too will visit Fort Michilimackinac at the tip of Michigan's lower peninsula. As you enter the barracks, the commandant's house, the church, the traders buildings, you, like me, may discover you have come on a pilgrimage.

D. G.

The Author-Artist

DIRK GRINGHUIS has been associated with the Forts of Mackinac since 1958. During that time he has written and illustrated four publications on the Mackinac region, has painted over 15 murals as well as illustrating countless works. This book is one of 28 books written and illustrated by him, half of them on Michigan history. He is also in his ninth year as producer-host for the television series, "Open Door to Michigan." He is the Curator of Exhibits at the Museum, and Associate Professor in Elementary Education at Michigan State University.

His latest works include: "Were-Wolves and Will-o-the-Wisps," "Lore of the Great Turtle," "The Great Parade," "Let's Color Michigan," "Let's Color Michigan Indians," and is working on a new book dealing with British folklore at Mackinac.

He holds special awards for his work on Michigan including the Governor's Award, A National Educational Television Award and an Award of Merit from the Michigan Historical Society. He is listed in Who's Who in the Midwest.

The End...

The Forts of Mackinac
Guide to official publications
Mackinac State Historic Parks

- **Mackinac Island — Its History in Pictures**
Over 360 historic photographs and drawings lavishly presented, depict the fascinating history of Mackinac Island.

- **France at Mackinac**
The fascinating story of French architecture, clothing, food and life as told in eighteenth century pictures and artifacts....... 44 pages.

- **At the Crossroads: Michilimackinac During the American Revolution**
British, Americans, and Indians clash for control of the upper Great Lakes, 279 pages. 210 illustrations, hardbound.

- **The Doctor's Secret Journal**
Frank revelations, amusing, shocking, but always fascinating, by Fort Michilimackinac's surgeon's mate 1769-1772...... 47 pages.

- **Attack at Michilimackinac — 1763**
The harrowing adventures of Alexander Henry, an eyewitness to the bloody Indian attack at Fort Michilimackinac .... 126 pages.

- **Treason? at Michilimackinac**
The version and sufferings of Robert Rogers as recorded in the official transcript of his trial for treason in 1768 .... 103 pages.

- **Soldiers of Mackinac Set A   4 prints**
Color prints suitable for framing of the 60th Regiment 1763, The King's Eighth 1775, Wayne's Legion 1796 and 1st Regiment of Artillery 1812.

- **Soldiers of Mackinac Set B   4 prints**
Mackinac Militiaman 1752, Chippewa Warrior 1763, 10th Royal Veteran 1812, and 10th Infantry 1882.

- **Mackinac in Restoration**
Twenty-five years of historic restoration, reconstruction and interpretation at the Straits of Mackinac. Illustrated......... 51 pages.

- **War 1812**
The exciting history of how the British, Indians and Americans fought for Mackinac Island from 1812 to 1815................. 43 pages.

- **Fort Michilimackinac Sketch Book**
Dramatic sketches depict the rich texture of Michigan's eighteenth century heritage.

- **The Young Voyageur**
For the young readers — A gripping historical novel about trade and treachery at Michilimackinac in 1763 .... 202 pages.

- **Lore of the Great Turtle**
Indian Legends of Mackinac retold and lavishly illustrated .... 96 pages.

- **Were-Wolves and Will-O-The Wisps**
French legends of Mackinac retold and richly illustrated .... 106 pages.

- **18th Century Military Buttons**
Recastings in pewter from original buttons excavated at Fort Michilimackinac and Fort Machinac.

- **Firearms on the Frontier: Guns at Fort Michilimackinac 1715-1781**
Gun parts excavated at Michilimackinac illustrated and described .... 39 pages.

- **Indian Costume at Mackinac**
Indian costume during the seventeenth and eighteenth centuries illustrated in color .... 12 pages

- **Reveille Till Taps**
Soldier life at Fort Mackinac, 1780-1895, told in words and pictures .... 116 pages.

- **Marquette Mission Site**
Archaeological excavation at the site of Father Marquette's mission in St. Ignace.................... 35 pages.

- **King's Men at Mackinac**
Sixteen British units 1780-1796 described and illustrated in full color .... 38 pages.

Mackinac State Historic Parks
Mackinaw City, MI 49701

L. SUPERIOR

Mackinac Island

Ft. Michilimackinac

Jacques Le Blanc

L'Arbre Croche

L. MICHIGAN

Danny O'Hara

Annette

The O'Hara

Sawaquot

Joe Loup